IR

ALSO BY GWEN COLE

COLD SUMMER
RIDE ON

Praise for *Cold Summer*

"*Cold Summer* is quietly intense, and filled with simple beauty. A story of a girl who has lost her place, a boy lost in time, and the universal pull to find home." —Kristen Simmons, author of *Article 5* and *Metaltown*

"A heart-wrenching ride through past and present, *Cold Summer* beautifully explores the bonds of family—the ones we're born into, and the ones we choose." —Sarah Marsh, author of *Fear the Drowning Deep*

"A poignant and heartfelt journey." —Wendy Higgins, *New York Times* bestselling author of the Sweet Evil series

"An addictive, emotional, deeply original, and beautifully-written time-travel tale that simultaneously offers up an engrossing plot and complex, real relationships. Just incredible! Read it." —Martina Boone, award-winning author of *Compulsion* and the Heirs of Watson Island trilogy

"There's no time like the present in this time-travel romance." —*Kirkus Reviews*

"*Cold Summer* is a romance at its heart—a true coming of age. The time travel element is a unique obstacle the lovers must overcome. . . . A good summer pick for fans of romance." —*Historical Novel Society*

Praise for *Ride On*

"A dusty, gritty, hair-raising adventure across a post-apocalyptic wasteland. It's impossible not to root for Cole's unlikely heroes." —Erin Bowman, author of *Vengeance Road* and *Retribution Rails*

"A starkly violent Western with surprising turns of tenderness." —*Kirkus Reviews*

"Nonstop action quickly turns the book into a page-turner and the well-drawn, complex characters are easy to like. The emotional maturity of the main characters adds depth to what could otherwise be a typical action-story plot and the romance, while understated, rings true. A richly drawn world provides a dim, gloomy context for a bright, intense story. VERDICT: Recommended as a first purchase." —*School Library Journal*

WINDSWEPT

A FANTASY NOVEL

GWEN COLE

SKY PONY PRESS
NEW YORK

Sky Pony Press books may be purchased in bulk at special discounts for sales promotion, corporate gifts, fund-raising, or educational purposes. Special editions can also be created to specifications. For details, contact the Special Sales Department, Sky Pony Press, 307 West 36th Street, 11th Floor, New York, NY 10018 or info@skyhorsepublishing.com.

Sky Pony® is a registered trademark of Skyhorse Publishing, Inc.®, a Delaware corporation.

Visit our website at www.skyponypress.com.

10 9 8 7 6 5 4 3 2 1

Library of Congress Cataloging-in-Publication Data is available on file.

Cover design by Daniel Brount
Cover photo credit: Getty Images

Print ISBN: 978-1-5107-4282-6
Ebook ISBN: 978-1-5107-4283-3

Printed in the United States of America

For Dad, because you never gave up.

SAM

NEW YORK, UNITED STATES

WHEN I CLOSED MY EYES, A PICTURE FLASHED IN my mind like a memory. It had appeared to me multiple times by now, but I'd never actually been there. A gray sky with a cliff, an ocean crashing below. Sometimes the sun was shining, sometimes not. Sometimes it seemed so real I could almost feel the breeze in my hair. Like if I only took a step forward, I could be there.

The roar of the subway brought me back to reality, to the echoes of people talking and someone playing music around the corner. I had roughly two minutes before my train would arrive. A few people were waiting along the platform beside me, but it was too early for the evening rush-hour crowd. Perfect for me—I hated being stuck in an overcrowded subway car.

The brisk October air sent shivers up my arms, and I pulled my beanie on to keep my hair in place, which was relatively short and always got in my eyes. I had decided to try bangs a month ago . . . never again.

I pulled my black earbuds from my bag and stuffed them in my ears, wanting to drown out the sounds of the trains and

1

people, but I didn't usually listen to anything. I just liked having them in so people who preferred small talk wouldn't talk to me, and I had an excuse to pretend like I couldn't hear them and ignore them if I had to.

I closed my eyes and pictured the cliffs again, imagining myself there.

A rush of wind wafted past, and I opened my eyes to find train windows flashing by. The doors slid open once the train had stopped. A few people stepped out, and I made my way into the nearly empty subway car to find a seat. It lurched forward as I took one near the door. I put my backpack on my lap and then pulled my beanie off because it was always uncomfortably warm in the cars.

I was about to start browsing on my phone when I noticed the person across from me, three seats down. He was looking the other way, absently fingering a messenger bag on his lap and staring at something in the empty corner. A dark jacket covered his gray hoodie, and the hood was pulled up over his head. I glanced at his shoes, which were a well-worn pair of Vans, because it's what I do—I look at people's shoes.

I felt odd staring at a complete stranger, but I couldn't help it. I'll be honest: he was *really, really good-looking*, as Derek Zoolander would say. Pieces of dark hair poked out of his hood—the same color as his eyebrows and lashes. Which then brought my gaze to his eyes, which—*wow*. He also had a great jaw and a neck I couldn't help but notice.

I didn't think even the cutest boy in my school was as good-looking as he was.

If Nella were here, I'd be texting her a GIF of a girl fanning herself.

A man walked by and I blinked away my focus. I looked down at my phone again and willed myself not to look up. A few popular girls in school had posted about a trip they took at the end of summer, and instead of examining their faces, I kept zooming in on the scenery—mountains, rivers, sometimes a skyline of an old European city. Just more places for my future to-visit list.

My eyes trailed to my left again, and my heart thumped when I saw that he was now staring at me. Not staring but *looking*. And on the subway, there was a big difference between the two.

His dark eyes held no aggression, and they certainly weren't hostile, unlike some people's on the subway. Having grown up in the area, I was already a subway pro, but I still had pepper spray for emergencies, and I never went anywhere without it.

Since staring at strangers was an awkward thing to do, I looked away, steadying my heart. I felt his eyes on me, but when I stole a glance, he was staring off in another direction.

I didn't think I was a slouch, but I also knew boys who looked like that didn't usually look at girls like me. Maybe I had something on my face? I took a subtle glance at my phone screen but couldn't see anything wrong.

I didn't look to my left for the rest of my train ride. When the doors finally opened, I took one last look as I stood, and he glanced up at me. A hint of a smile tugged at the corners of his mouth.

His eyes made my stomach constrict. It took everything I had to make myself turn away and walk out onto the platform. The cold air nipped at my neck and I had a weird desire to stay on the train. It was usually the opposite. I hated the train and always wanted to leave as soon as possible.

Maybe because I was hoping he would say something.

I glanced back in time to see the train pulling away and the strange boy giving me the same odd smile. It made heat rush to my cheeks, and I suddenly felt stupid about feeling so flustered about an attractive stranger.

The train disappeared, but still, I stood there unmoving. I forced myself to take a step forward and then another and walked back up to street level, where fall was coming all too quickly. My head felt too cold, and I was about to put my hat back on when I realized—I had left it on the train. I kept walking, cursing stupid, cute boys who made me forget my favorite hat.

I turned onto our street and couldn't wait to get inside and away from the cold. Before my parents were married, my mom made my dad promise that they would someday live on a street lined with brownstone duplexes and aged trees that grew along the sidewalks. She got what she wanted this past summer when we moved literally one mile west from our old house. Our street was quiet for the most part, inhabited only by elderly people and couples with no children and little barking dogs.

I hurried up the steps and went inside, wanting to rid myself of the chill in my bones. Levi greeted me inside, tail wagging and ears folded back, ready for me to pet him.

"Have you been a good boy today?" He was just over a year old, so the question was always relevant. Once I found an entire bag of Doritos flattened and licked clean on the kitchen floor. I gave him a good rub behind his large German shepherd ears and then let him out the back door to do his business.

Before going upstairs, I grabbed a cheese stick from the fridge, then I made my way up the three flights of stairs to my room. I was usually home alone for the first couple of hours after school and I had tons of homework to do, even though watching reruns of my favorite sitcom sounded way better.

"Sam?"

I blinked awake and stared at the ceiling. The light coming through the window was dim, warning me of the coming evening. I was splayed over my bed where I had apparently fallen asleep, but it was so comfortable that I didn't want to get up.

"Sam? Are you up there?" Mom's voice echoed from downstairs, and I sat up groggily, swinging my legs over the side of the bed. My head spun a little before I could see straight.

"Yeah, I'm here!" I glanced out the window and wondered how long I'd been out for.

"All right, I just wanted to make sure you're home," she said and let out a laugh. "You're so quiet, I never know."

I smiled even though she couldn't see me, knowing exactly *why* I was quiet. "I'm just working on my homework."

"Well, I've already started dinner, and it should be done soon. I'll call you when it's ready."

I heard her walk away from the bottom steps and toward the kitchen. My books were untouched on the comforter next to me, but still, I ignored them. I ran my fingers through my hair and pulled it into a small ponytail. Most of the shorter layers didn't stay up, but I didn't bother trying to keep it that way.

I slid off my bed and wandered over to my desk. Even though it was a bit too dark to see the different shades on the jigsaw pieces, I scanned over one section quickly and fitted one of the pieces where it belonged.

The picture was beginning to form into a harbor somewhere in Greece, and the blue was the utmost amazing shade. I stared at the one missing piece of the sky where the point of a tower should have been.

I still couldn't find it and it bothered me to no end. I had the desire to get down on my hands and knees and search for it on the floor. Maybe I would later.

A car door shut outside our house, and I peeked out my window to see Dad down below, coming up the stairs from the street. Mom greeted him and their muffled voices drifted from below and Levi's dog tags rattled as he tried to get them to play with him. Unlike the rest of the dogs in our neighborhood, Levi never barked and I loved him more for it.

A couple walked past on the sidewalk—neighbors from down the street—and then something else moved across the road, catching my gaze. There was someone leaning against one of the trees with his hands shoved deep into the pockets of his jeans. A hood covered most of his hair, but I could tell it was dark, almost black.

"Sam, dinner's ready!"

I flinched and looked toward my bedroom door. A shiver ran over my skin, and I couldn't help but look out the window again.

He was gone. I searched the dark streets, saw no one, and came back to the place I'd seen him seconds earlier. The only movement was some leaves blowing across the sidewalk, as though they were trailing after something invisible.

My heart hammered as I made my way downstairs. The lamps were on, making the house feel warmer than it did earlier in the day, but I felt more uneasy than usual. When I came to the bottom floor, my eyes flickered toward the front door, and I had the urge to either look out of it or lock it. I shook my head—I had probably just imagined him.

My parents were already seated at the table when I entered the room. Mom startled when she saw me in the doorway.

"Gosh, Sam, I didn't hear you come down." She held her hand over her chest. Since she always took her contacts out whenever she got home, she was wearing her glasses, and her dark hair was done up in a messy knot.

I smiled and looked down at my socks, thinking they *were* a bit too silent. "Sorry, I didn't know I was being *sneaky*," I said, taking my seat.

"It's all right," she said, shaking her head, "you just take after your dad."

6

Right on cue, Dad looked up from his plate and grinned widely. "Don't worry, Sam, it's a gift. You can sneak up on your mom and scare the daylights out of her. It's fun."

"And maybe your dad should watch *his* back more often," Mom muttered as she stabbed some pasta with her fork, but she smiled back at him.

I smiled at my parents' light banter and listened to them quietly throughout dinner. I loved these nights; just the three of us around the table, talking about our days. Occasionally, one of them would bring up an old memory of when I was still a kid, and we would get a laugh.

But not tonight. I felt like only half of me was present, still distracted by what had happened just before dinner. It may just have been my mind playing tricks on me, just like the cliffs that kept popping into my head whenever I closed my eyes.

"So how's your last year of school going?" Mom asked. "We haven't had the chance to talk much lately."

We rarely got the chance to sit down to dinners during the school year—with my schedule and both my parents working full-time, it was hard to do more than once a week, if we were lucky.

I pushed my food around on my plate. "It's fine." I shrugged. "It feels just like how school felt before. Just a different commute."

"So in other words, you still hate it?" she asked.

"*Hate* is a strong word, but something close to that?" Mom didn't catch my sarcasm, so I just smiled and said, "It's fine, really."

"Are you still okay riding the subway?" Dad asked. Our old house was right next to the school, so I had walked every day, but now that I was riding the subway, Dad wouldn't stop asking about it.

The mention of the subway made my stomach do a little flip when I thought of that guy again. And as I thought of

7

him, another clear picture formed in my mind, and just as before, it was of somewhere I'd never been.

It was a park, almost dark with the sun going down. Someone sat on a bench near a pond, and an old willow stood nearby, stretching its limbs over the water. The stranger sitting on the bench had his hood pulled up, shadowing his face so I couldn't see him. Something tickled the back of my mind, and my stomach fluttered again.

It was like a snapshot as quick as it came.

I looked up and both my parents were waiting expectantly, like I hadn't spoken for a couple of minutes even though it had been only a few seconds.

"No, it's fine," I answered, trying to rid the image from my head. "It's actually a lot better than I thought it would be." I stood and took my plate to the sink. "I should go finish my homework."

Mom glanced at me. "You mean *start* your homework?"

I gave her an inch of a smile and made my way back up to my room. Everything was dark, and I felt around for my bed-side lamp, trying to avoid bumping into my bed. I clicked it on, and the light illuminated my cozy room. My schoolbooks still sat untouched on my bed, but instead of cracking them open, I went to my window and looked down on my street.

Nobody was out there. The street was damp and quiet, and I wondered if I *had* imagined it all. I couldn't help but think that the person in the street earlier resembled the guy from the subway. The image of those cliffs came to mind, so clearly like before, and I thought that maybe that was all he was.

Just my imagination.

REID

NEW YORK, UNITED STATES

I SAW HER FOR THE FIRST TIME A WEEK AGO.

The wind was brutal that day, and her hair kept blowing across her face. I only caught a glance before someone bumped into my shoulder and nearly knocked me down. I only caught sight of her retreating back disappearing into the subway station. She was pretty—that's all I remembered thinking.

And now today, by chance, I saw her again.

I'd been sitting for ten minutes before she came and took a seat across from me. I couldn't believe it. The chances of seeing the same person in New York City twice in the same week are less than none.

Initially, I looked over just to see who was there, and it was her, already staring at me. It wasn't my fault I was having a bad hair day, but maybe it was worse than I had thought. But then I remembered I had my hood on, so that couldn't be it. There was no way I could just stare back, so I tried to give her a smile. I had never been good at smiling, but I attempted one anyway. One side of my mouth turned up . . . I think.

I don't think it worked.

When she looked away, I knew it was a lost cause, because at first glance, there were some immediate differences between us. Bluetooth earbuds were in her ears and she glanced at her phone often, whereas I didn't even *own* a phone. From the bulkiness of her bag, I could tell there were schoolbooks hidden inside. I was a dropout.

I could count on one hand how many people knew I existed, and it was fewer than four, one of them being a best friend who was barely ever around. And another who was like a half brother, but I rarely saw him either.

The train came to a stop.

I glanced over to see her leave. As the doors shut, I had already accepted that I would never see her again, but something happened that I wasn't anticipating. I expected her to keep walking, never to think of me again—after all, I was just a stranger on a train.

Instead, the girl stopped on the platform and turned back to look at me. It was the most unexpected thing, and in my nervousness, I gave her one last feeble attempt of a smile, so she knew I saw her. The train lurched forward, and I lost sight of her as the tunnel swallowed me.

The lights flickered, and with a glance to her empty seat, I saw a hat lying there. Had it been there before? Was it hers? I couldn't remember if she was wearing one when she sat down.

I made a split-second decision. Besides, I had nothing else to do. Hell, I was riding the train *because* I had nothing else to do. It was either ride the subway more or roam the streets— decisions, decisions.

The hat now gave me a reason to say something to her. It gave me a reason to *see* her again and, in that moment, I knew I wanted to see the stranger from the train. Even if just to learn her name.

I grabbed the hat, closed my eyes, and when I opened them, I was standing on the subway platform the train had just departed from. People stood around, waiting for the next train to arrive. Of course, no one noticed me appear. They never did unless they happened *not* to be looking at their phones or staring at the empty space I suddenly came to inhabit. I pulled the strap of my bag over my head and across my chest, then started for the exit. My eyes scanned the crowd frantically as I moved, then I caught sight of the girl at the top of the escalator.

I started after her, but with too many people in front of me, I had to wait my turn to go up the escalator. She got up to the street before I did, and then I had to fight through a group of school kids before I caught sight of her turning the corner. I quickened my pace to catch up.

She took a left and started down a more residential street with trees lining the sidewalks. It was a nice neighborhood. Not expensive or fancy, but somewhere in between. I was about to call out to her when she turned up a set of steps and disappeared inside.

I stopped, hat still in hand. It would be really weird now if I knocked on the door. *Hey, I'm that stranger from the subway and I happen to know where you live now.* Yeah, not creepy *at all*.

I tucked the hat inside my bag, thinking maybe I'd come back later. Maybe leave it on her doorstep with a letter.

No, that would be even weirder.

So, without anything else to do, I drifted.

A little before five thirty, I came back to the front of her house and leaned against one of the old oaks across the street. It was dusk, but the house was still relatively dark inside. There were lights on in the living room, but the top half was still dim and shadowy. I didn't know what I was doing there, and I didn't have any reasons other than the hat in my bag.

A small car turned onto the street and parallel parked almost effortlessly in front of the house. A middle-aged man climbed out. He had to be her father. His hair was just as dark as hers, not yet showing signs of gray, but he wore glasses. He never gave me a glance as he walked inside.

I knew I should have just left. I couldn't stand outside her house forever and hope to "run into" her again. I glanced at her house one last time and saw a face peering out of the top window.

It was her, and she was looking right at me.

It was only for a moment, and then something distracted her attention behind her, and that's when I made my break. I was gone before my heart took another beat and my stomach flipped. I never had to think about drifting anymore. It came without effort, as easily as breathing. I was gone long before she even turned around again, leaving but a slight breeze as any proof that I had ever been there.

The park was deathly quiet when I appeared, and the old bench was cold as I sat down, placing my bag next to me on the seat. Minutes rolled on, and I tried to occupy my mind until I would be tired enough to go home and sleep.

An evident breeze warned me I wasn't alone, but I also didn't have to worry. Just as I said, I could count on one hand how many people knew I existed, but there were only two who I still saw on occasion.

"You look sad sitting there like that. You know that, right?" Jake's Australian accent interrupted the silence, but I smiled anyway. He came around the front of the bench and shoved my bag aside to make room for himself. His hair was extremely messy, as usual, half of it pulled into a bun, and he wore a worn leather jacket. He smelled like expensive cigars.

"I haven't seen you since last month. Did you get lost in Japan?" I asked.

He shrugged. "Only for about a week."

I laughed because it was a joke. Drifters never got lost.

"Do you have a house there now?" I glanced at him sideways. "Maybe I should check it out."

"I just got one yesterday actually," he said, glancing at me, "but we both know you won't be stopping in."

"Sure, I will." My sarcasm was all too obvious, and I rolled my eyes.

Jake's smile disappeared. "What are you doing here?"

"I'm sitting, stupid. What does it look like?"

"Reid." Jake's voice was on that serious line that he rarely used, and I knew he was going somewhere I didn't want to. "I mean, what are you doing *here*? You can go anywhere in the world, and yet you choose to stay here. I don't see the point." He shook his head. "Sometimes I don't understand you."

I stared out at the water and knew I needed to change the subject.

"You coming this weekend?" I asked.

Jake shot me a glare but answered, "*You* shouldn't even go. You're getting yourself in deeper every time you do. It's not safe and you know it."

I waited, knowing the rest of his answer was coming.

He finally said, "Yeah, I'll be there, but just to see you get your ass kicked."

"You wish."

His smile disappeared again. "You know you have to stop soon, Reid. One of these times, I won't be there to bail you out. They'll find out about you soon enough."

He was in one of those *moods* and I hated it.

"Well, until then, it's the only thing I can do."

"No, it's the only thing you *will* do."

I stood up in a rush and turned to face him. "Because it's the only thing I *know*, Jake! I'm not like you. I don't steal things that aren't mine. You take advantage of too much."

13

"And you take advantage of nothing. We don't have this ability just to do nothing with it. I don't know about you, mate, but I want to actually live my life. You?" He gestured toward me. "You act like you don't even have one."

"I'm living, too, just in a different way. Why can't you just accept that I'm not the same as you?"

Jake stood and I hated having to look up at him. "Oh yeah? Where *are* you living these days? The last time I saw you, you *weren't*."

"I found a place."

"You found a place?" he mimicked. "Does it come with a loo?"

I glared at him as best I could. "I get by just fine. I don't need you to tell me what to do."

"Sometimes it seems I do." His eyes searched me, and I felt exposed.

I clenched my jaw and grabbed my bag, slinging it across my chest. "I'll see you around."

I was about to drift when he caught hold of my arm. "Reid, I've told you before, you're welcome to stay at my place. I mean it."

"Which one? I don't fancy Paris as much as you do."

He smiled crookedly. "You know I have one here, too, and I always will." He let go of my arm. "I'll see you this weekend. Try not to get lost until then."

Jake disappeared before I did, and by then I realized I didn't know where I was going. I didn't lie when I'd said I found a place, because I did. I just didn't want to go there yet.

So I just went wherever my mind took me.

SAM

NEW YORK, UNITED STATES

THE FOG DISAPPEARED OVERNIGHT, AND THE morning came with the sun shining into my bedroom. My alarm clock went off five minutes earlier, but I still had plenty of time to get to school. I sat on the edge of my mattress and stared at the floor, trying to wake up.

Last night's dreams were still playing vividly in my head, and I wanted nothing more than for them to be gone. It was the third night in a row that I had strange dreams, but they were only strange because they had an unnervingly real feeling about them.

My cell phone vibrated on my nightstand, and I reached over to see who it was. Nella, my best and basically only friend, from school had texted me. We used to be neighbors, but it was different now that there was more distance between us. In more ways than one.

I opened her text.

Meet me at the café after school? It's been forever.

I quickly texted her back and told her yes. I rarely did anything after school, not to mention *outside* of school, but Nella was the one person I never minded hanging out with. We were both similar in our introverted ways, and I was pretty sure that was the reason we were friends.

Since I was still good on time, I pulled my laptop from under the bed. It was Dad's old Apple laptop, so it took a little while for it to come to life. After checking my usual social media and glancing at gossip, I opened FaceTime and clicked on the only contact I ever called—my older brother, Logan.

He answered after just two rings, his face filling the screen. I hadn't seen him in person since the summer, but he hadn't changed much, though it seemed like he needed to shave.

"Hey, Sam." He smiled and ran his hand through his hair like he had just gotten up, which he probably had. The rest of his room was dimly lit behind him, and I saw his messy bed in the corner.

"Hey, sorry I missed your last call," I told him.

"That's what happens when you become a senior. It's even worse when you're in college, trust me." He grinned. "How's that going, by the way? School, I mean, is it as horrible as always?"

"Well, I wouldn't use the word *horrible,* but close enough. Will you be here for Thanksgiving?"

"Yeah, I'm pretty sure I'll be able to make it," he said, pulling on a T-shirt. "If not, it'll be Christmas for sure."

"Well, I think plane tickets are kinda cheap right now."

Logan smiled and shook his head. "Getting there isn't a problem, Sam, don't worry."

I narrowed my eyes. "What are you going to do, walk? You *are* off school that week, right?"

"Don't worry about it, I'll get there. It just depends if I get bombarded with homework the week before."

I sighed. "Okay."

Logan stared at me through the screen. "Are you doing all right?"

16

In that moment, I thought about being open and telling him about my weird dreams and images of a cliff that I couldn't get rid of. That I woke feeling unrested and had been experiencing weird flashes of places I'd never been to. That I saw a boy disappear on a sidewalk. But no, I couldn't tell him those things.

It was probably just school stress, or something.

"Yeah, I'm fine," I lied.

School dragged by. The air was still brisk and seemed to be getting colder by the hour. Once the school day was over and my bag was full of schoolbooks and homework, I started walking the two blocks to the small café where I would meet Nella. There was a bite to the air, and I could almost make out the fog from my breath. It was the coldest day yet since the leaves had started to change colors, and the season was ending too soon.

I missed my hat. I was angry that I'd forgotten it on the train.

After I had walked another block, the small café finally came into view. It sat on the corner of a three-way intersection next to a park, and it always seemed to be overlooked, sitting between a popular Starbucks and a Panera Bread. I didn't know how the café stayed open, but it was a nice getaway to those who, like me, appreciated silence.

Nella, already seated at the table near the front window, waved when she caught sight of me. A younger couple sat at the other table near the opposite wall. Otherwise, it was empty. I walked across the worn wooden floors and sat down across from Nella.

"We have to do something this weekend, Sam," she announced. "It's been forever since we've hung out."

"Since school started, which was only about a month ago." I smiled and finished with, "And hello to you, too."

She glared levelly at me. Her dark hair was pulled back into a simple ponytail, and she was wearing her glasses, as usual. She looked cute with them on, not to mention smart, but she hated to be reminded of them. Her poor eyesight was the bane of her existence.

"I need to do something besides school," she said. "Can't you agree just this once?"

"When has there been a chance for me to *not* agree? We both know we never do anything anyway."

She finally broke out a smile. "That's why we're friends— we're both boring people, and both perfectly fine with that."

"So why the sudden change in mood?" I asked, taking off my jacket.

She shrugged her shoulders and sat back in her chair. "I just feel like doing something. I need to get out once in a while."

The barista made her way over from the counter with our drinks and smiled brightly at us. "It's good to see you girls again. You haven't been here in a while."

Nella smiled back. "We've been super busy with school. You guys aren't going under because of us, are you? Because I really think I would die if I had to start going to Starbucks." Her eyes widened with fright, and I laughed.

She chuckled and shook her head. Her blonde hair was thrown up into a messy knot and it bobbed along with it. "No, we're doing just fine. Let me know if you need anything else."

Once she walked away, Nella shook her head at my cup. "I still don't understand how you can live without coffee."

I cupped my hands around the mug and smelled the delicious chocolate and whipped cream. "Because coffee is disgusting, and I'm not going to argue that point again."

"Fine," she answered tiredly. "But seriously, Sam, we're doing something this weekend. Is Friday night good for you?"

"Friday? But—" I tried quickly to think of an excuse, but

I came up with nothing that would satisfy her. Homework couldn't be one, because I would have all weekend to do it. And because she asked three days in advance, Nella knew for a fact that I didn't have prior plans. The only image that came to mind was my unfinished puzzle and multiple episodes of an anime to watch, and that wouldn't be a good enough excuse for Nella to back down.

She smiled at me over her mug. "I thought so. I'll pick you up at nine, and you better be ready."

"*Nine?* Where are we going at nine o'clock at night?"

Who goes out at nine at night? Actually, a lot of people, but none of them being me. That was an hour before I was usually in bed.

I could just imagine it now: Nella and me getting lost somewhere in East Harlem with no way home. It would be raining and cold, and our phones would be dead.

But she was right—going out could be fun, once in a while. I smirked. "Fine. Nine it is."

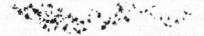

By the time Nella and I parted ways from the café, it was nearly rush hour. The crowds were already thick as I made my way down the steps into the subway. I hated crowds, but sometimes there was no way around it in the city. I was tempted to shove my earbuds in to drown out the noise with actual music, but the train was already slowing down and I was short on time. People jostled their way in and out of the doors, and I just barely got through before they slid shut.

I glanced around for an empty seat, but they all seemed to be taken. Some people were already standing, hanging on to the handrails above and the bars in the middle of the car, but I didn't really feel like standing.

I started down the aisle, desperately searching for an empty place I could cram into. My eyes trailed toward the back, where I spotted two empty seats along the wall. I made my way back, watching my feet so I wouldn't trip over anything and being especially mindful that my backpack didn't hit anyone, but when I looked up again, only one seat was left.

The guy from yesterday sat in the other.

I stopped moving and just stared at him, my heart giving me a little kick. He was wearing the same jacket and hoodie, but today his hood was down, showing his dark hair, messy like the day was too windy for it. Should I sit next to him? Our *encounter* from yesterday had been on my mind throughout the day, but I had been almost certain I would never see him again. The chances of that happening were close to none, and yet here he was.

I tried to make myself breathe and then continued toward the empty seat casually. He glanced at me as I sat down but said nothing, looking away before I knew it. He looked awkward sitting there; he was stiff as a board and just stared straight ahead. I stared straight ahead, too. My heart beat too fast and I felt heat rise to my face.

Why does it always have to be so hot on the train?

I glanced at him from my periphery, tracing over him without making my head move an inch. His nose, his mouth, and then I looked at his eyes . . . his eyelashes.

I looked away, wondering if I should say something. I *wanted* to say something, but what?

Hey, I think you're . . . cool-looking? Yeah, right.

The subway suddenly felt unbearably hot and crowded, but I didn't want to leave. If my subway ride had lasted forever, I wouldn't have minded. The only thing I wanted was for him to notice me, or maybe he had and he was just avoiding me. Which was worse? Did he even remember me from yesterday?

Then he finally tilted his head toward me, and I bravely looked up in return.

"So . . ." he paused for a moment, and out of the corner of my eye I could see his chest rising and falling. "Is this going to become a regular thing?" His voice was nice—had the smallest rasp to it on the back end.

A regular thing? I had no idea what he was talking about, but then it dawned on me.

"Oh, here?" *He actually remembers me.* I smiled shortly and looked over at him again. I had a hard time breathing when I did. His eyes were a soft brown, like velvet. They stared straight into mine. "I think the odds are against us," I said, distracted.

"Maybe, or maybe we can see what happens tomorrow." A smile crept into his lips.

I could barely breathe.

"I guess we'll see then."

"I guess so," he answered. There was something about him, something that . . . my parents wouldn't approve of. Ugh, I hated even thinking the words. But it was there. Something unknown that made my heart race.

Then my stop came, and I had to get off. I stood reluctantly and was about to leave when he said, "Wait."

I looked back and he was holding out my hat.

"You forgot it yesterday," he offered.

I went to take it, and we both held onto it for a moment too long, the hat suspended between us like an offering.

He finally let it go and I said thanks.

"You're welcome."

I left just before the doors closed.

We looked at each other through the window again as the train pulled away, and I secretly and stupidly couldn't wait until the next day.

SAM

NEW YORK, UNITED STATES

I FOUND THE MISSING PIECE! THE TIP OF THE tower was finished, and I saw now that it was more tower than sky, rather than what I'd originally thought. I felt a small feeling of completeness now that I had the whole top half done. I always went from top to bottom—I didn't know why.

"Sam? You awake?" Mom asked from the floor below me. I could hear her shuffling around in her bedroom. Dad left early this morning before I'd even woken.

"Yeah, I'm up," I half-yelled back.

She peeked inside my door. "Sam, I actually need to talk to you."

"Okay. What about?" I pulled on my hoodie and started putting my bag together. She walked over and sat on the edge of my bed.

"We decided to take an early anniversary trip this week."

I turned to her, raising an eyebrow. "And where are you going?"

Mom shrugged, smiling. "He said he wanted it to be a surprise."

"*Oooooh!*" I was excited for them, and yet I still had an uneasy feeling in my stomach, the one that had been around for a few days now, something I couldn't quite put my finger on or find a name for. But I kept my happy face on for her, knowing how much the trip meant. They hadn't been able to go away together in years.

"So you're okay with it?" she asked. "You know I'll always change my plans if you need me to."

I shook my head and finished packing my bag. "No, it's fine, really. Besides, Levi will be here." I turned, swinging my bag onto my back. "I think it's good. When will you be leaving?"

"Early Friday morning." Mom stood and started to leave, pausing at my door. "You have a good day, all right? I'll see you tonight."

I nodded and she left. The door closed downstairs and Levi's collar rattled softly as he walked back into the kitchen. As I stood there, needing to get to school, I caught sight of myself in the mirror. My hair was again pulled back into the smallest ponytail with the rest of the short strands hanging over my ears and around my face. My bangs would need a trim soon, but since I wasn't a fan of them, it would mean growing them out, which was always awkward. I wasn't sure which option was worse.

Everything familiar stared back, and I silently wondered what the guy from the train thought about me. I wasn't flashy or stylish—I was just me.

Meanwhile, he could have been on some sort of magazine cover or maybe a self-made Instagram star, especially with those eyelashes. I blushed—whoever and whatever he was, he would have to either take me the way I was . . . or not at all.

Somehow the odds of that possibility seemed too great, and yet I dared to hope just the same. I pushed down the self-doubt and tried to be confident about myself and how I looked, so I gave my reflection a small approving nod.

Today was the same as the day before—sunny and cold, but for once the weather was the least of my worries. The only thing my mind could wrap around was my upcoming subway ride and, for the first time, how much I was looking forward to it. School dragged on, as always, and my eyes constantly found the clock, marking down the minutes and hours. I was glad when it was finally over.

I wanted to see him again. I had already admitted that fact to myself before I had gone to sleep the night before. I wanted to see him again.

I was nearly running by the time I got to the station with my heart pounding, and my stomach felt uneasy again. The anticipation was killing me. By the time I reached the stairs, the roar of the subway was already in my ears. It bounced off the cement walls of the tunnel, and it felt as though I was entering a dragon's cave. I let the adrenaline sink in, almost thriving on it, and hurried down the steps.

The knots in my stomach got worse by the second, and I suddenly started doubting the whole situation over again. Should I just walk home? What if he wasn't on the train? I didn't have time to worry about it. I headed to the last train car and boarded with a few others.

I spotted him instantly, because how could I not?

The doors slid shut behind me and I walked over, taking a seat directly across from him. A smile slipped into the corners of his mouth, and he glanced at the few people around us before coming over to sit next to me.

"The view is better over here," he said.

I glanced at the wall full of ads that he gestured to and smiled.

"Right."

"So," he started, "I guess the odds are better than we thought."

"Or maybe you're stalking me."

His eyes narrowed and one side of his mouth went up. "That would be hard since I was on the train before you."

"I suppose that's a good point." But still . . . it's hard to believe it's just a coincidence, isn't it?

"Have *you* ever stalked someone?" he asked, turning just a little more to face me. "It seems like you don't know a lot on the subject."

I smirked. "And you *do* know a lot about the subject?"

He shook his head, his dark hair shifting a little over his forehead. "It's not part of my skill set. And if it was, I'm not sure I would tell anyone."

"What *is* in your skill set?" I asked.

His gaze drifted away as he thought about it. When he turned back, he asked, "Do you have a piece of paper?"

I opened my bag and tore a piece out of my Moleskine notebook without thinking twice. I handed it to him, and he said, "Perfect."

While he was busy tearing the paper into a square, I asked, "So what brings you onto my train—job, school, tourist?"

He shrugged, his eyes on the paper. "Nah, I just felt like it."

"You *felt* like it? Nobody just feels like riding the subway."

"And why is that?" he inquired, his eyes glancing up.

I felt my face twist into something close to disdain. "Because it's the subway. It's small and crowded, and it usually smells like rotten chicken."

"Maybe, but I still enjoy it. Have you ever ridden the subway just to see where it takes you? You go underground one street, and the next time you come out, you could be almost anywhere." He smiled crookedly again, and I wondered when I would see a full smile from him and what it would look like. I could tell it had to be amazing from the little pieces I kept seeing. "That's what I like about it," he continued. "I'm guessing you have an actual reason to be here, since you beg to differ."

I nodded, letting his reason sink in, thinking that it didn't sound so bad. I'd never ridden the subway for no reason, but now I sort of wanted to. I didn't get out of the city much, but I always had the desire to go to different places. The problem was that I never liked traveling. Planes were just as bad as subways, and cars drove too slowly for my liking. There was no source of transportation that I truly liked.

But maybe this would be a good place to start. Just exploring my own city some more.

"I have to ride it because of school." And then I asked, because I couldn't hold in it any longer, "You've really done that before?"

"Done what?" His fingers started folding the paper and I tried my best not to stare, seeing how gentle and precise they were.

I cleared my throat, and my thoughts, and said, "Ride the subway for fun?"

His fingers paused folding and he glanced at the floor in front of us, thinking. Then he looked at me again and nodded. "Yeah, sometimes I get on one train just to get on another, never really looking at where it's taking me."

After a pause, he asked, "What do you like to do for fun?"

"I can't tell you."

"Why is that?"

"Because you'll think I'm boring."

"Then we'd be on the same page," he replied.

"You think you're boring?" I raised an eyebrow, thinking there was probably nothing boring about him.

"I'm riding the subway for the heck of it. What other proof do you need?"

He had a point. "Well, I like jigsaw puzzles and watching anime."

The boy smiled crookedly at me, and my heart rate jumped again. "What are you, retired?" he joked and then immediately

26

said, "I'm sorry, that was a joke. Sometimes my sarcasm doesn't translate."

"Oh, really? I didn't pick up on it."

We shared a smirk.

Then the train started slowing down, and it was already time to get off. He seemed to know it, too, frowning slightly.

"Your stop?"

I nodded. To be honest, right then I had no idea what to do. Obviously, I wanted to see him again, but I also didn't want to ask for his number. What if he said no?

"Here." He held out the paper, which had turned into a tiny origami elephant. I took it carefully, afraid to bend it and mess it up.

"See?" he said. "I'm boring, too."

"Anything but boring."

"I was thinking the same."

Even though his words were simple, he meant for them to be more.

I stood, still cupping the little elephant in my palm.

"See you tomorrow," he said.

My stomach tossed and I nodded. "Tomorrow."

REID

MAINE, UNITED STATES

I WOULD SEE HER AGAIN TODAY. I COULDN'T STOP thinking that I would, but it never seemed real enough. I felt so foolish when I talked to her; I had no idea what I was doing. I tried to be smooth and composed, but underneath, where my heartbeat and my stomach stirred, everything seemed to be on fire, on fire *while* riding a roller coaster.

I didn't know how to talk to girls, especially ones I liked.

The more I thought about it, the more I realized I'd never liked a girl this much before. Which seemed stupid and foolish since we were strangers on a train with nothing more than a handful of exchanged words between us.

I stared out across the bay, and the fresh scent of coffee reached my nose. The bell to the café somewhere behind me kept dinging as people went in and out. My stomach growled, but I kept my eyes on the dark water below. I'd decided last night that I would surprise her by meeting her on the train in the morning. She would expect me later in the day, but I knew I couldn't wait that long. I thought about how carefully she held the elephant in her palm after I handed it to her, like it was

28

something precious. Stupidly, I thought about how her hand would feel in mine.

Then I felt like I was being creepy, for already thinking about holding her hand. I hated having chunks of days where I had nothing to do. Time gave my mind room to roam around memories I didn't want to have or ones I wanted to forget. It was easy to push them away when I was occupied, but times like these were torture.

If I closed my eyes, I would see things that haunted me. If I thought about things too deeply, something large would crawl up my throat and stay there, not willing to go away until I forced it to. I needed to always be doing something.

"Hey, this is a private dock," a voice called behind me.

I looked over my shoulder and saw a man standing there, holding his cup of coffee and wearing a crisp suit. Maybe he owned one of the fancy yachts I was standing too close to. Adults were always suspicious about teenage loiterers being up to no good. My rugged appearance probably never helped.

"My father owns one," I said over my shoulder.

"Yeah, which one?" he challenged, not believing me for a second.

God, he was annoying. I turned and walked past him, heading toward the road.

"Hey, kid!"

I could hear him walking after me. The soles of his shoes were loud on the dock, whereas mine were silent. When I got up to the road and turned around the corner of the café, I could have sighed in relief. Suddenly, the sound of the man's shoes and the smell of the ocean in Portland were replaced by the roar of the subway and the scent of polluted air from the hundreds of taxi cabs above me on the streets of New York.

Right about now, the man would turn the corner and nothing but a brick wall would stare back at him.

The side of my mouth lifted at the thought of his confused face. There was nothing like spending a morning in Portland, screwing with annoying rich men.

I wasn't sure what train she would be on in the morning, so I waited where I could see the stairs. A few minutes passed, and then I saw her coming down from the sidewalk above. She wore the same knitted beanie I'd returned to her over her short hair, and her cheeks were pink from the cold morning air. If I waited any longer, she would see me, so I focused on the arriving train. It was about a minute away. I quickly drifted to the opposite end of the car where she always sat.

By the time the train stopped, it took everything I had to keep my leg from bouncing nervously. What if she had decided she didn't like me? And even more, what would happen if we went further than this? My question was left hanging as the doors opened.

I watched her walk in and take a quick sweep of the people around her, but she didn't notice me, didn't know to look for me. Her eyes lingered on the place we had been sitting for the last two days—maybe just a coincidence, and then she took a seat down near the other end, brushing some of her hair away from her face. The moment she turned, I stood from my seat and walked over.

I slid smoothly into the seat next to hers and sat back, placing my bag on my lap. She still didn't notice that it was me. She seemed to be thinking deeply about something, her eyes staring into the corner but looking at nothing.

Being close to her again made my heart pound. Her soft scent filled my nose: laundry detergent and something I couldn't place. Whatever it was, I couldn't get enough of it.

An extreme wave of doubt suddenly washed over me, and I almost bolted for it right then. Did it actually make me a stalker now that I was seeing her on the morning train, too?

Did I seem too desperate? How could I be so stupid to ever think I could pull this off?

I was about to make a break for it and abandon my place, but then she looked at me and it was too late. She nearly jumped at the sight of me next to her, but I couldn't mistake the small smile when she realized it was me. Suddenly my self-doubt melted away and all I knew was that I had to try to get her to smile like that again. Maybe this wasn't a mistake after all.

"Hi," she said.

"Hi."

"I didn't expect to see you this morning."

"Well, I'm sorry for the disappointment." It took everything I had to keep my voice calm. I was just as nervous as I had been the day before.

She shook her head. "No, I'm not disappointed. Just . . . surprised." Her eyes flickered over once before she asked, "Seriously, how do you keep doing this?"

"Keep doing what?" I couldn't help but smile.

I could have sworn I saw her blush a little.

"You keep finding me. How do you do it? There are like, dozens of trains."

"Have you always had your hair short?" I asked instead of answering.

"You're changing the subject." She narrowed her eyes, but I could tell that she wasn't mad or annoyed.

"Because I'm avoiding the question."

When was the last time I smiled so much? The action felt odd and out of place but not wrong. Like my mouth wasn't used to doing this totally normal thing and had to relearn it.

She answered me anyway, "Yes, ever since I was ten, or something. It's just easier. But you can't keep avoiding the question forever."

31

"So you ride the subway for school, right? How long have you done that?" I started again.

She hesitated and I wondered how long I could keep up this charade. "Yeah, I used to live within walking distance, but we moved houses over the summer."

Her hands absently played with the hat in her lap, and I glanced at her fingers and thought about the elephant I had made her again and how gently she held it. I shifted straighter in my seat and cleared my throat.

"But you don't like it," I said. "School, I mean."

"Is it that obvious?" She sighed. "I can deal with it, though. It's my last year, that's all I have to get through."

"And then what?" I studied her as she stared ahead, her eyes wandering. "Do you know what you're going to do after school?"

"No." It was a simple answer, but even I could tell there was a complexity behind the word. The subject seemed to deflate her and I quickly responded, "Well, make sure you do something just for you, and not anybody else."

She looked over at me. "Is that what *you're* doing?"

"Every damn day."

The train slowed and her eyes dropped as she gathered her bag. She stood but paused before heading for the door, which had only seconds until it would open.

"Will I see you again later?" she asked.

I didn't want to come across as some desperate guy who had nothing better to do (I didn't), but that wasn't something I wanted her to know. I also couldn't say no, though.

"Do you want to see me again?"

The doors opened and she hesitated a fraction longer. Her eyes met mine.

"Yes." A small smile appeared right before she left, and I savored it.

The doors closed. Sinking deeper into my chair, I let out

a long breath. The nervousness finally left my stomach and I could breathe properly again. I hoped the strange something between us would become something more. I wanted to know her name, but the moment never seemed right to ask.

Now I had to wait another seven hours before I could see her again.

By the time the train pulled into the next stop, I was gone. My seat sat empty and nobody looked twice for the boy who had been there only moments ago.

The task of wasting time.

It was something I'd come to loathe. It was the only thing that ever made me think twice about going back to school, but even then, it was never enough. Occasionally, I would slip into a big class somewhere in a community college and nobody would ever even notice me. And if they did, it wouldn't matter anyway.

But today was worse than usual, because I had something to actually look forward to. I sat in the park for as long as I could take it, which turned out to be close to an hour. It had to be a personal best. After that fun little hour of boredom, I walked to the other corner of the park, near Sixth Avenue. I enjoyed the walk—it was a change from the ordinary.

I almost felt like a normal person, walking. Walking under the colored trees, the sun shining down through the branches, I was in oddly good mood. *Maybe I'll ask her what her name is.* I knew I probably wouldn't do it, though. I was still too nervous. But tomorrow . . . that could be a real possibility. Tomorrow had a good feeling to it. I smiled again, and then my stomach stirred with doubt.

Maybe.

But to kill time, I decided to see what Iceland was like this time of year.

SAM

NEW YORK, UNITED STATES

HE WAS ON THE SUBWAY AGAIN THAT AFTER-
noon. We made more small talk about nothing important,
and even though the subjects were uninteresting, I found him
to be anything but. My heart fluttered against my rib cage
every time he looked at me. I felt my cheeks redden every time
a hint of a smile appeared.

I felt like a complete idiot. Was this what other girls in my
school felt like when they were around boys they liked? I was
beginning to understand why most of them had boyfriends. I
loved having his attention, and I wanted to know more about
him. Even the empty, meaningless stuff.

Now I stood waiting for the train after school on Friday. I
was slightly disappointed I hadn't seen him that morning, and
I found my general feelings toward the subway had drastically
changed—I actually looked forward to riding it now.

I tried to take my mind off him and thought about the
planned night out with Nella. My parents had left early that
morning, and I had the house to myself for the next few days, if
not more. All I had to do was remember to feed Levi and make

sure my homework was done. Flickers of green cliffs flashed through my mind briefly and I pushed them away. Last night's dreams had been horribly vivid, and I was almost to the point where I wished they would stop. They weren't normal, and whenever I thought about them, they put me on edge.

When the subway doors slid open, I walked on and took my seat next to the boy whose name I still didn't know. I watched his fingers play with the edges of his bag, and then he suddenly asked, "Can I walk you home today?"

My heart sped up in response to the unexpected question. I didn't even know his name, and he was asking if he could walk me home. Did I want a stranger knowing where I lived? The answer was simple.

"No." The spark in his eyes faded, but he nodded, understanding. Then I compromised. "Not the whole way at least."

"How many blocks?" The corner of his mouth lifted, just as it always did.

"That's for me to decide," I said.

"More than one?" His tone was close to joking and I laughed.

"Possibly."

"I'll Rock Paper Scissors you for it. If I win, I'll walk you at *least* halfway. If you win, you get to decide when to ditch me."

His eyes smiled, and I couldn't say no.

I won; two out of three.

We stood as the train came to a stop, and I swung my bag around my shoulders. Now that our relationship had moved from beyond the train and into the real world, I was determined to find out actual real-world facts about him. We were still strangers to each other, but I had a feeling that was about to change, and this was the first step. He followed me onto the platform, and I had to remember how to walk. But I had only gone about five feet when I stopped and turned to him.

"I think this would all work better if I knew your name. That way if my parents ever ask about you, I won't have to say, 'the stranger from the subway.' Because I'm *pretty* sure that wouldn't go over very well."

"And why would you be talking to your parents about me?" He cocked his head curiously, raising his eyebrows. I blushed. "Did you just admit that you want to see more of me?" He was holding back a smile and it made me blush even more.

And then something happened, something I had yet to see. He grinned, widely, and when he did, a dimple appeared on his left cheek.

Needless to say, I was distracted.

"I—no, it's just—I want to know your name." I spoke like I didn't know how to form words properly.

"I think it's more than that, but I'll let it go for now." He looked past me for a moment before telling me. "My name is Reid."

"Sam."

"Good. I'm no longer *the stranger from the subway*."

"Now you're Reid, from the subway."

"I'm not sure if that's any better, to be honest."

I smiled and walked up the steps with Reid at my side. The sun started to dip below the city horizon when we got to street level. Seeing the sun low reminded me again that Nella and I had plans tonight, which I didn't want to think about yet. "Can I ask you something?"

He shrugged. "I don't see why not."

"What do you do?"

Reid glanced over. "How do you mean?"

"You said you were riding the subway because you felt like it. What else do you do? Do you go to school?"

He hesitated. "Um, no."

"A job?"

"No."

I slowed to a stop. "Then what do you do?" People walked past, giving us dirty looks for stopping the flow.

"I go places," he answered simply.

"Like what kind of places?"

He narrowed his eyes, didn't answer, and walked away, leaving me no choice but to follow him. When I came up beside him, he said, "Wherever I want. Why are you so curious?"

"Because I don't think you're telling me the whole truth." There were only a few more blocks until my street, but I wanted to know at least *something* about him before we parted ways. I knew his name, and that was it. It wasn't enough.

"You're right . . . I'm not." There was disappointment in his voice. Something flashed in his eyes before he looked away, like a pang of guilt, or something very close to that. A normal person would have elaborated and explained himself, but he didn't.

I didn't feel like smiling anymore. I stopped walking at the corner of the next street. I felt a pang in my stomach now and had the desire to go home. "Well, thanks for walking me—not home." I avoided looking into his eyes.

"Did I say something wrong?"

"No, it's what you didn't say. I'm sorry, it's just going to be hard learning more about you if you're never going to tell me anything of substance. I know we just met, but it seems you don't want to take this any further."

I was surprised that my words came out sounding so strong. I didn't feel strong. I felt terrible because I didn't want this good thing between us to go away, but I had known sooner or later whether what we shared on the train was going to end. Eventually, you have to get off the train. Eventually, you reach a destination.

His eyes weren't happy anymore, and I was thinking the tone of my voice might have been a little too harsh. I wasn't making it easy on him, but I didn't care at that point. He was going to either like me or hate me, and he could have it be his choice. Besides, I tried to convince myself, he's just a stranger, so what does it really matter?

Because I want to know the stranger.

"It's not that I don't want to tell you things, it's that . . . I can't right now. We only just met." His eyes became pleading. "Please, ask something else, anything, and I promise to tell you the truth."

I didn't know what to ask, but then something popped into my mind. I bit my lip, not sure if I was going too far from my sanity. But if I never asked, I would regret it.

"Were you in front of my house Monday night?"

His eyes froze, and I could almost see his brain working out the question. I was afraid of the answer but still wanted it all the same.

Reid opened his mouth, but a moment passed before he said, "Yes."

My mind couldn't come up with any possibilities. "Why were you there? How do you know where I live?" I could only imagine the shocked look on my face.

"I was trying to give back your hat, but by the time I caught up with you, I saw you go into your house." He cut himself off, even though I felt like there was more to it. His chest began rising and falling faster than before, and he took a step back and then raised his palms. "I'm sorry—I'll just go."

"Reid, wait." I didn't want him to go yet. I was worried that if he left now, I wouldn't see him again. I shouldn't have cared so much, but I did. Despite everything, I still wanted more.

"I promise you won't see me again. I'm sorry—" He turned and briskly walked away.

"Reid, wait!" I watched him disappear around the next corner. Tears stung the corners of my eyes, and my stomach took a nasty dip.

The rest of my walk home was a blur, and I opened the door to my house before I knew it. Levi came trotting from the direction of the kitchen, his tail swinging high to greet me, but for once, I wasn't in the mood to give him even a simple smile. I let him outside, and once he was back in, I went up to my room.

I didn't want to think about anything for the next three hours until Nella came over, so I decided the best thing to do was sleep. Sleep and hope that I hadn't ruined everything.

It was quarter to nine when I walked downstairs. My hair was pulled back in a messy ponytail and I had just thrown on a simple cardigan and a black jacket over it. I hoped Nella wouldn't want to go anywhere fancy. Everything I wore matched my mood.

Levi was already at the bottom of the steps, ready to follow me into the kitchen. We normally left him inside while we were gone because he had a good temper and usually just slept, but I decided to let him explore the backyard until I got home. I probably wouldn't be gone that long.

I watched for a moment while he ran around our small yard before I locked the back door. The house seemed eerie without my parents around, and I almost felt like flipping on the TV so there would be something to fill the silence.

I sat on the bottom step to wait for Nella. It was dark outside, and probably cold, but thankfully there was no wind. Reid kept coming to mind, and my heart sank every time he did. I messed up, or maybe I didn't and it was better this way, but it *felt* like a mess-up.

When he said I would never see him again, I felt like he'd been telling the truth, like he really meant it. I wanted to take

39

back everything I'd said. I wanted to tell him that I didn't care if I didn't know anything about him—it was okay if he was really just trying to give my hat back on Monday.

I groaned into my hands, angry for both feeling miserable over a boy I barely knew and for letting such a boy go so easily.

A car horn honked outside, and I hurried out the door, glad for any distraction tonight. Nella was driving her mom's blue Mini Cooper, and I climbed into the passenger seat. The interior was already warm, and Nella stared at me as I buckled my seatbelt.

"*What?*" I asked.

"What are you wearing?" she asked dramatically. She pushed the gas a little too hard, and we were on our way.

I glanced over her clothes and took note of her nonwrinkled pants and red trench coat, which probably hid a blouse underneath. I shrugged. "What I usually wear? You didn't say anything about dressing up."

She shook her head. "I should have known. How will a guy look twice at you if he mistakes you for a boy at first glance?"

"*Nell.*"

"Sorry," she muttered, "I didn't mean that. At least that jacket is cute."

The mention of guys brought Reid back into my head, and for some reason, I suddenly felt like staying home. Despite wanting a distraction, I also didn't want to be in public. I wanted anime and pity food.

"I don't look that bad, and you know it. Where are we going anyway?" I asked.

"Well, I don't know if I should tell you, because you'll probably jump out of the car if I do."

I glared over at her. "Nell, where are we going?"

She peeked over at me as we stopped at a red light. "Well, there's this club—"

"A *club*? We aren't twenty-one. How are we supposed to get in?" Not to mention, I had never *been* to a club and didn't know if I even ever wanted to. My life just got more lame with that thought.

"It's in an old warehouse—"

My mind drew a blank until the meaning of what she'd said dawned on me. "Is this club . . . *legal?*" I crossed my arms and glared even more. First she dragged me out of the house, and now she was taking me to an illegal club.

"Come on, Sam, where's your fun side? Besides, it *is* going to be fun. That's the point of tonight, right?"

I put on my bored face and asked dully, "How so, exactly?"

"I heard they have the best DJ in the city and the bartender doesn't card anyone. Not to mention, the bouncers don't card anyone at the door because they don't care."

"We don't drink. And you know dancing really isn't my thing."

"I know, but I haven't gotten to the best part yet."

I watched the road, and we were already getting closer to some part of town that I probably would have avoided if I hadn't agreed to go with her. I wasn't just afraid for us; I was also afraid for her mom's car.

As Nella continued her argument, she said something I never expected to hear: "They also hold fights there."

My eyes widened looking at her again, forgetting about the deadly neighborhood.

"This club that we are going to, *right now*, is also a fight club?" I clenched my jaw together so I wouldn't issue dirty words at my best friend.

She shrugged and grinned at me. "Yeah, I guess so. It seems pretty awesome to me."

"Have you been taking drugs lately . . . or like maybe you're on them *right now*? Seriously, Nella, what has been up with you?

You're not usually like this. We don't go out Friday nights, and we definitely don't do clubs."

Even as I said it, I knew that wasn't true. She had been slowly changing over the year, and I had simply decided to ignore it. She was changing while I stayed the same. The thought itself didn't help boost my self-esteem. She was moving forward without me.

A moment passed before she spoke, but when she did, there was something about her voice that sounded different. "I met someone."

The car was silent for a whole minute until I asked, "Why didn't you tell me?"

"I didn't tell you because it only happened within the last few days. Actually—I think you have a class with him. His name is Luke."

I blinked. "I know Luke. He's in English with me, right? Is he the blond guy that looks like Tamaki from *Ouran High School Host Club* except with glasses?"

She snorted. "I don't even know what you're talking about, but sure? Please don't be mad at me, Sam. He said he was going tonight, and well . . . I couldn't say no. Please don't be mad at me?"

I shook my head. "No, I'm not mad at you—just tell me next time, okay?"

She nodded, smiling. "I promise."

We drove on—to who knows where, and I didn't want to ask—and the traffic had died down by the time we were surrounded by old warehouses. There were a few cars in front of us, a few behind, and we figured they were going to the same place. Why else would people be out here?

We arrived, and I felt like going home again. A red light flashed in my brain, reminding me I was way out of my comfort zone, and I sank deeper into my seat.

A line had formed outside the door. It took us at least five minutes just to find parking a couple blocks away, and I made sure that Nella put any valuables out of sight and locked the car before we started walking. Despite the cold weather, a couple of girls passed us wearing high stilettos and miniskirts.

"I so don't belong here," I muttered.

Nella didn't even glance at me, continuing to walk with the same persistence, no doubt finding Luke was on her mind. "That's not true."

Liar.

We waited in line for a good twenty minutes before we reached the door and the bouncers just glanced at us as they let us in, one of them frowning at what I was wearing. The building was packed full of people, and the bass of the music vibrated through the floor. It was the loudest, most chaotic place I'd ever been to.

Couples were grinding each other on the dance floor, moving with the beat and lights. Their limbs seemed to move separately from their bodies, and the only thing I could focus on were their shoes. A lot of high heels and boots mixed with expensive loafers cluttered the dance floor. It made me feel even more out of place with my worn Vans.

The air itself smelled like alcohol and sweat mixed with a strong scent of cologne and perfume. I wrinkled my nose—another reason never to go to these places.

"Sam!" Nella yelled into my ear, but I could barely hear her. "I'm going to go find Luke, okay?" I nodded. "I'll text you when I find him."

I sighed as she walked away, leaving me to the elements. I could have gone with her, but it would have been harder trying to follow her through the crowd. I looked around and saw nothing I wanted to do. The bar was not an option, and I knew I would be repelled by everything over there, including the guys who scouted every girl that walked past them.

I leaned against a pillar and simply watched the chaos. Out of a dozen people, one guy walked by wearing a pair of skater shoes. I gave him a mental smile. Another guy glanced at me as he walked by, and then he backed up with a hopeful smile on his face.

"No."

His eyes flashed at my abruptness, but he continued walking. I hated being here, and every time someone looked at me, I thought of Reid. Of how nothing but butterflies attacked my stomach when he looked at me, and how differently I felt about him than anyone else. How could I miss someone I barely knew?

The music stopped abruptly, and people made their way off the dance floor, forming a loose circle around the large area. I craned my head to see why, but I couldn't get a glimpse. A few more lights turned on, making everything brighter, hinting at something about to happen.

I pushed my way through the crowd to get a better view and finally made it toward the front. A girl stood in front of me, but I could see just over her shoulder. A man stood in the center of the former dance floor, listing rules into a mic. He wore a tight T-shirt that barely contained his biceps.

This must have been the fight club Nella mentioned. Everyone seemed excited for it, while I was afraid the cops were going to burst through the doors at any moment and arrest everyone. Maybe I watched too many movies, but still, it seemed plausible enough for me to believe it could happen.

The man stopped yelling, and an even bigger guy walked out onto the floor, taking off his shirt and shoes and throwing them aside. He wasn't really huge, but he had a way about him that made me feel sorry for whoever was going to fight him. The man speaking into the mic looked into the crowd behind him for the other fighter. When he saw someone, he yelled at him to come up, only with harsher words than I would like to repeat.

The crowd became impatient. I tried to spot Nella and couldn't see her anywhere. Then a few of the people around me chuckled at something. I turned my attention back to the floor and everything just stopped—the noise, my breathing, maybe even my heart for a moment.

The second fighter was Reid.

SAM

NEW YORK, UNITED STATES

HE SLIPPED FROM THE CROWD LIKE A SHADOW, and I stared at him as if someone had slapped me. My heart was the only thing I could feel, because every other part of me seemed numb with shock. He pulled off his T-shirt, along with his Vans, leaving me looking at a boy with loose-hanging jeans around his hips and an expression that made my blood run fast.

I finally blinked and took a deep breath. I thought I would *never* see him again anywhere, let alone *here*.

People yelled, eager for the fight to start and to see some action. Girls eyed the two fighters while their dates busied themselves making bets, exchanging cash over people's heads. While the referee spoke to the bigger man, a stranger walked up behind Reid and talked into his ear. He was probably a few years older, with a stylish man-bun and sporting a black leather jacket.

Reid stared at the floor as his friend spoke, nodding at whatever he said. I found satisfaction in watching him— the way he spoke and nodded, interacting with his natural environment.

I forced myself to look away—mostly to give my heart a break because it *just wouldn't stop pounding*. People pressed in around me and it was almost claustrophobic, but my want for escape disappeared when I heard the sickening thud of a punch.

Everyone yelled for more as I looked up to see the other man wearing an angry scowl, ignoring the cut along his jaw-line. Then everything happened quickly. Reid came at him again, fists held close to his head like he actually knew what he was doing—wearing an evil little smirk on his face. That's when his opponent came at him like a storm. He wasn't just big—he was fast.

His first punch to Reid's jaw made me cringe. The blow snapped his head back, almost knocking him off-balance. The fight didn't seem to be in his favor. The man was all over him, hitting him over and over in the ribs and then again in the head. I hadn't realized my own fists were balled until my palms started to hurt where my fingernails had dug in. I didn't want to watch him lose, and I didn't like seeing him get hurt.

Reid took one more hit, then stepped back to wipe the blood off his mouth. Between his last hit and before the other man came forward, I thought I saw something. Reid glanced to his nameless friend behind him, lifting the corner of his mouth, which baffled me, because why would someone smile while losing a fight?

The man came up behind him, and I worried Reid wouldn't see him in time. But then he turned as the man's fist drove toward his face. He moved so quickly that I didn't even see it happen.

It was like he was there, and then magically, he was just four inches to the left.

I looked around to see if anyone else had noticed, but it seemed I was alone in my confusion. Maybe nothing *had* happened; maybe he was just that *fast*.

The man tried to punch Reid again, almost immediately, probably thinking he had just missed, but the same thing happened. Reid evaded him like it was the simplest thing in the world, and my mind kept trying to catch his movements.

If he was just fast, I should have still been able to see something, a shift of his feet, a tug at his shoulders, anything. But each time, like a blink, it was though space and time simply adjusted him *slightly* out of the path of his opponents' fists. Like a glitch in a video game.

The fight shifted, and Reid took back control. Every time he swung, he was dead-on, making the other man stumble, and I wondered what had changed in Reid to make him suddenly so good. Everyone else noticed the change, too. They were surprised with the suddenness of it but welcomed it all the same. More entertainment. Everyone screamed for more. Reid stepped around the guy's punches, hitting him every time in return, but his movements were too quick, so effortless. It was almost unnatural.

My eyes trailed away from the fight, and I found his friend on the other side of the circle. For some reason, he didn't look happy about the direction of the fight, which puzzled me. His arms were crossed over his chest, watching the fight like he *wanted* Reid to lose. He turned his head, looking up toward the balcony, and I followed his gaze.

Three men looked down on the fight, and just from one glance, I knew they were trouble. They looked *angry*, and not angry like my parents were when Levi pooped in the house as a puppy—these guys looked murderous. They were the type of people, if I ever saw them walking toward me, I'd cross the street to get away from. The cheering suddenly became louder, and my attention was dragged back to the fight. Reid was the only one left standing. The other man lay unconscious on the floor.

He had won.

Reid finally smiled and turned back to his friend, who didn't return the gesture. People still yelled and screamed; a few even passed money to each other, paying out their bets. I couldn't help but smile, too; he'd been more than amazing.

Reid, somehow, eventually caught sight of me in the crowd and he froze. His wide grin slowly turned downward, like he couldn't believe what he saw. I wanted to somehow cross the room full of people to get to him, but my feet stayed planted where they were. Reid gave me a quick, secret smile before finally breaking eye contact.

It wasn't enough.

He pulled on his shoes and T-shirt while people patted his back. The next fight was about to start. Everyone was ready for more, but I couldn't watch another fight knowing he was here. I wanted to go to him and talk and maybe apologize. I wanted to start over, to go back to the ease of what we'd shared on the train. He disappeared through the crowd, and I started to push my way toward him as people gave me dirty looks.

"Sam!" I turned to see Nella coming toward me with Luke right behind her. I tried to smile, to hide my disappointment—I wanted to find Reid—but Nella's joyful face made me ashamed that I would put my best friend on the back burner for a guy. All she wanted to do was have me meet Luke officially. I could do that . . . and *then* I would find Reid.

"Sam, this is Luke, but I think you already know each other." Nella barely glanced at me—the boy beside her had her undivided attention.

Luke nodded at me. "We have English together, right?"

"Yeah." I tried to smile, but I couldn't stand there a moment longer being a third wheel. "Actually, Nell, I think I saw someone I know. I'll catch up with you later, all right?"

She looked at me, unsure of my words because we both knew that I didn't know very many people. But she let it go, because the boy who clung to her arm was too irresistible to give up. "Okay, I'll text you when we're ready to go." They walked away before I could even nod.

I took off in a fast walk, heading toward the opposite wall. I was too nervous to breathe properly, and I had to remind myself how to keep my legs moving. What if he still didn't want to see me? We had parted on such bad terms that I wished we could start over. But the smile he'd given me moments before made me think maybe there was hope.

Maybe I still had another chance.

The new fight must have been at a high point, because everyone started yelling louder. People pushed past me to get to the crowd from the bar, and it got easier to move when I was closer to the outer wall where fewer people stood. I started glancing around for him, knowing he should be there somewhere. What would I say when I saw him?

I didn't have any time to think of an answer before I found him. He fit in here, with his black T-shirt and hair that would make any girl blush. People talked to him like he'd just won the lottery, and a few girls hung around him, trying to gain his attention.

The group of people finally left him alone, but after summoning up enough courage to start walking again, I stopped short. Three men approached Reid, and the smile was wiped from his face. They were the same men who'd been watching the fight from the balcony. One of them grasped Reid's shoulder a little too hard and whispered into his ear. Before Reid could respond, they turned and walked toward the side exit, Reid between them looking all too small.

My stomach churned as they disappeared through the door. Nobody else seemed to notice them leave. Nobody but me. I glanced around, thinking if I could find Reid's friend he could help, but there were so many people, and I had a bad feeling in my gut that every second I wasted was one second too many.

I moved without thinking about what I was going to do, took a deep breath, and opened the door where Reid and the men had disappeared. The shouting from inside the club disrupted the quiet night, and I quickly shut the door, hoping the noise wasn't loud enough to carry too far. A dim light shone above the door, making me feel exposed, so I quickly stepped into the shadows in case anyone was looking.

Voices drifted from my right and I tentatively walked forward. It wasn't long before I saw them under another floodlight. I couldn't move another step or they would be sure to spot me. *What was I doing?*

Their voices drifted to me again, but the man's voice was too low and hushed. I shouldn't be here. I took a step back, and my shoe knocked a rock aside, just loud enough for someone to hear.

"Hey!" A voice rang through the night, and I did nothing but freeze in response. A man I hadn't seen before—way too close for comfort—came toward me, and all the others, including Reid, turned to look in my direction. I caught Reid's eyes and saw something in them that confirmed I shouldn't be there. I took another step back, ready to make a dash for the door.

The guy stood about twenty feet away, just enough distance between us so I could get to the door, but the moment I turned, a large hand grabbed the back of my jacket. It tightened and spun me around, his other hand wrapping around my arm so I couldn't move.

"Well, look what I found," he said into my ear. "Lost?"

"Bring her over here, Wallace," the other man called, a little older than everyone else, maybe somewhere in his thirties.

Wallace shoved me into a walk, so I had no choice but to comply. He stopped me in front of the man. I stared at his jacket and tried to keep my breathing normal.

"Who are you?"

I hesitantly opened my mouth, but the man, Wallace, shook me hard from behind, obviously impatient. "I—I'm sorry, I didn't mean to come out here. The club was just too hot and I was trying to find Reid."

"She's nobody, Buck," Reid's voice echoed from where he stood. I quickly glanced at him. His body was stiff beside the other man, and after my eyes trailed down, I saw why. There was a knife pressing against his ribcage.

I had to force myself to breathe. *Don't freak out, don't freak out.*

What was Reid doing with these people? Was he in a gang? I shouldn't have followed him outside. I should have called for help or told Nella where I was going or taken the time to find Reid's friend.

"Do you know her?" Buck asked, glancing at Reid.

"I just met her inside. We barely know each other." After a moment of silence, he added, more hushed, "She doesn't know anything."

Buck turned his attention to me again, and I could smell the cigarette smoke on his clothes. I didn't know what Reid was talking about, but whatever he said was true. I didn't know what was going on, and clearly, I knew even less about him than I thought I did.

When the man spoke, he wasn't talking to me, which was a relief because my mouth was too dry to form any sort of response.

"Reid, if you're lying to me, and she's one of *you*, things could get very ugly."

"I'm not lying."

Soft footsteps came from behind us, and Buck shifted his eyes to the newcomer. Wallace didn't move, so I couldn't see who it was, but I hoped it was the police, even though something told me I wasn't so lucky.

"Causing more trouble, Buck?" The voice had a thick Australian accent and its words didn't even hold a hint of fear.

"I wondered when you would show. Reid has trouble staying in line, and if you didn't have horrible timing, I would have shown him a thing or two."

The Aussie appeared in my peripheral vision. I recognized him as Reid's friend who had talked to him before the fight. He kept his distance, and Reid stared at his feet, like he was ashamed that his friend had to come pull him out of trouble. I wasn't going to complain though; relief flooded through me at the sight of him. Maybe things were going to be okay.

"Trust me, Reid's telling the truth. She's nobody. Just bad timing, yeah? I don't think there's a drifter in this entire city that you don't know about, isn't that right?"

"You talk too much, Jake. This isn't your problem."

"But it becomes my problem if you're going to hurt my friend."

Buck smiled over at Reid. "He deserves what he gets."

Jake was suddenly serious, his mouth formed into a hard line instead of an easygoing smirk. "Just let the girl go back inside. She's not part of this."

Buck nodded to Wallace, who shoved me in the direction of the door and then pointed over my shoulder with a knife I hadn't even seen until then. I shuddered, glancing at Reid again. He wasn't looking at me.

"Get walking, girl. Be more careful where you wander next time . . . and maybe pick your guys better."

He didn't have to tell me twice. My legs were shaking as I left. I hated leaving Reid, but my fear of staying was stronger, and at least he wasn't alone anymore. His friend seemed to know how to get him out of trouble.

But as I left, I still stupidly couldn't help but wonder: *Would I see him again?*

REID

NEW YORK, UNITED STATES

AS I WATCHED SAM WALK AWAY, I KNEW THE SECond chance I'd almost gotten with her had been blown. There was no way she would want to see me again, not after what she'd just seen. Besides, what girl would want to date a guy who rode the subway for fun, took part in illegal fight clubs, and ended the day with a knife held to his ribs?

No wonder she didn't look back.

Dempsey roughly smacked the back of my head, bringing my attention back to Buck. I got the feeling he'd been staring for more than a moment.

"Now, where were we?" Buck gave me a wicked smile. I knew exactly where we were before Sam had come along—they were about to show me a *good time*. Dempsey put more pressure on his knife and it broke skin, making me flinch. Buck seemed to enjoy it, as always.

"In my defense, you never told me that I couldn't come here," I said hurriedly. "I didn't know it was yours." The first part was true at least. I was just hoping they wouldn't be here tonight. I risked it because I needed the money.

"You should know that we own every fight club from here to Chicago. What do I have to do to get that into your brain? Must I drill a hole and shove a note inside?"

Somehow, I hid any reaction. "I hate to correct you, but you said to stay out of *Chicago*, not New York. And I haven't seen you guys since then, so I figured it was fair game here." True, true, and false. I really should have stopped lying before I got myself into even more trouble.

"It was implied," Buck replied with a scowl. I watched his fingers ball into a fist. "I hate seeing your face around here, and I think it's about time I do something about that."

Jake stepped forward. "Look, Buck, he obviously didn't mean any harm tonight. Why don't you let him go with a warning, all right?"

"If I let him go with a warning, he'll just keep doing it. What are you going to do, babysit him? If I were you, I would forget that you've ever met him and get lost."

Buck glanced at me again and I wondered if I'd finally gone too far. I'd known not to come, and what I was getting myself into. Why couldn't I take my own advice or live with the consequences of my actions?

"Let him go this once," Jake offered. "If he does it again, then it's fair game. But I promise, it'll be the last time."

I knew Jake hated doing this. The way he said his words made me think this really was the last time he would stick his neck out to get me out of trouble. I'd never realized how much I depended on him to bail me out.

"Did you hear that, Reid?" Buck slowly turned to face me again. He smiled when he caught sight of my blood on Dempsey's knife. "The next time I see you fighting, it better be in some alley where I don't give a shit. You got that?"

I nodded. Dempsey shoved me to the side, but not before

digging his hand into my pocket and pulling out the wad of cash I won tonight.

"That's *mine*." I made to grab for it, but Dempsey flashed his knife again.

"Try to get it—the moment you drift, you're dead." He winked at me as he walked past.

My stomach growled, reminding me that I hadn't eaten in the last day. I couldn't do anything to get the money back, though. Dempsey would see me coming. I clenched my fists because it was the only thing I could do.

"Consider this your apology for messing up and showing your face," Buck said, smiling wider. "You've caused us too much trouble already."

"That's his money, Buck," Jake interrupted. "He won it fair."

"You think *that* was a fair fight?"

"The rules were read, and there was nothing said about drifting."

Buck laughed with no humor. "Maybe we should add it to the list then." They turned and walked away. Jake stared at me like I was the stupidest person he had ever met.

"*What?*" I didn't wait for an answer, bending down to grab my jacket. My skin was cold, and not just from the air, so I shrugged it on, pulling the hood over my head. "Just spit out whatever you're going to say."

He shook his head. "Not here. Come back to my place, and if you don't come, I'll never come looking for you again. Your choice." He left before saying another word, leaving nothing behind but a small breeze, like an exhale. I glanced toward the club door again, wondering if Sam was still inside. Even if she was, she wouldn't want to talk to me. I'd lost my chance.

I sighed, brought Jake's apartment to mind, and drifted. He popped the cap of a beer when I appeared there, still scowling. His place was the same as I remembered. Huge windows lined the wall, and the living room was too big to be called a living room. His black Harley sat directly behind his couch. I was more of a Ducati fan myself and I always liked to remind him of that.

"Drop your stuff. You're staying here tonight."

"No, thanks."

Jake drifted from the kitchen right onto his couch. Papers flew off his coffee table and onto the hardwood floor, but he ignored them. "I wasn't asking. You're staying here tonight because you're my friend, and I need someone to play Xbox with, and because you owe me for saving your ass."

"You have online friends you can play with. What about that Nostradamus guy?" I dropped my bag where I stood, taking my place on the couch. The leather was cool but smelled good as always. Every time he offered me a place here, a little piece of me got closer to just giving in.

After a little while, Jake asked, "That girl, was she really nobody? I can't have you lying to me like you lie to everyone else."

"I don't lie to you. And . . . she's not nobody."

"But she doesn't know anything. I could tell by her face that she had no idea what was going on."

"I barely know her, and it's not like it matters now anyway. Not after what she saw."

Jake shrugged and finished off his beer. "You never know."

"I doubt it."

"How're your ribs?" Jake asked.

I shifted uncomfortably, not wanting to be reminded of it. "They're fine, he didn't dig too deep."

"But next time he will. I'm not stupid, mate. I know there will be a next time because your dumb ass can't seem to stay away."

"I'll start going to the smaller bars again." They didn't bring in as much money as the bigger clubs, but I didn't have much of a choice anymore. Buck and his goons seemed to be everywhere and money wasn't worth anything if I was dead.

"Or, you could stop altogether. What is it with you and fighting? Do you take joy in getting hit on a regular basis?"

I touched my jaw where it was tender and winced. I tended to heal fast, but this injury would take a bit longer. It would have been easier to win the fight without being hit at all. And it would have been easy to pull off, but there was less money if the fight wasn't long enough to be entertaining.

"Jake, please, don't go into this again."

"How can we not talk about it? I'm worried about you, Reid. You know what Knox likes to do to drifters who get in his way. One of these days, you're going to find yourself bolted, and I won't be able to help you."

I shivered hearing his words, knowing that it could be true. "You don't have to get me out of anything anymore. If something does happen . . . it'll be my own fault, and I'll deserve whatever comes to me."

"Then make sure you don't do anything stupid. How are you going to get to know that girl if you die?"

When I looked at Jake, he smirked like an idiot.

I said, "That girl isn't going to ever want to see me again."

"How do you know that if you don't *try* to see her again?"

"She's not going to want to see me."

"And why not?"

I opened my mouth but closed it. There were too many reasons to name. The question should have been, *Why would she?* I had no answer to that.

"Reid, did I ever tell you of the girl I met in Toronto?" Jake pulled off his jacket, throwing it on the floor.

I shook my head. "I never knew you met *any* girls." I grinned as he narrowed his eyes at my sarcasm. I was actually surprised he didn't already have one at the apartment for the night.

"Just shut your mouth and listen. There was this girl in Toronto last year. We hit it off at a party, and I couldn't seem to stop going back to her. I was in that city more than anywhere else. It was like I kept being pulled back there." Jake shifted his eyes onto me. "I even told her about me, and she didn't freak out or call the police."

That got my attention. "You told her?"

"It's not like there are drifter police, Reid. You tell people who you trust, or someone you want to see a lot more of. There's no way you can even *begin* a relationship without telling them the truth. It can't start with lies."

"So . . . you're saying I should just tell her?" The pit of my stomach ached with nerves. I never thought I would tell *anyone*.

"Yeah. And you never know," he said with a shrug, "maybe she'll be all right with everything."

What if she was? What if she still wanted to see me? A little spark started my heart with the possibility of seeing more of her. It was hard not getting my hopes up.

"What happened to that girl in Toronto?"

"She found someone else. It was nice while it lasted though, you know? Telling someone, I mean. Just do it. You never know how it'll turn out until you do."

I nodded, already thinking about the possible outcomes. It had never occurred to me to just tell someone before. I always thought it would become a problem if I did. There were two outcomes. The first would be her screaming and running away, probably calling the police in the process. The second would be her staring at me until she convinced herself that she wasn't crazy, and neither was I.

She would see me as who I was.

"Okay, I'm sick of talking. Let's play." Jake stood and grabbed a controller, throwing me an extra. He turned on his seventy-two-inch flat screen, and the next hour was a blur. Sometime after midnight, Jake disappeared into his room, and he told me to eat whatever I could find. That was the first time I took him up on his offer. My stomach was full of nothing and I needed food.

Around two in the morning, I stood on his balcony, stomach full of carbs, not at all tired. The streets below were still alive, and I had an unearthly desire to drop down and disappear. I could have, too. I wouldn't go splat like any other person thinking they could fly.

I could enjoy the ride without the consequences.

But where would I go? I had the whole world to choose from, and yet I had nowhere I truly wanted to be. I could go to the hottest club in L.A. or go wedding crashing in Paris. The freedom that thrived within me was never-ending. I lived off it.

But New York was where I lived because it was never silent. It was the opposite of the home I grew up in. The home I could never think about. When I was in New York . . . I didn't feel so alone all the time.

I needed to figure out when to see Sam again, even though she might not want to after what had happened outside of that club, and even though I told her she would never see me again, I knew I had to. I'd never wanted to tell someone about drifting so much in my life, and I wondered how she would react.

There was only one way to find out.

SAM

NEW YORK, UNITED STATES

NELLA DROPPED ME OFF A LITTLE AFTER MID-night. The house was quiet and undisturbed. I shivered before making my way down the dark hallway, turning on a few lights as I went.

Levi was waiting to be let in by the back door, and he followed me to the stairs, taking his place at the bottom as I went up to my room. My parents' bedroom, the second level, was dark, which made me realize—this would be my first ever night alone in the new house.

The origami elephant Reid made for me sat on my night-stand, bringing a little warmth into the room and making me think about him.

My mind was numbed by the night's events, and Reid's face wouldn't stay out of my head. But on top of everything, I felt like I was getting sick. My stomach tossed and an ache was coming from somewhere deep within me. I went to bed curled up under my blankets, hating the cold sheets and wishing they were warmer.

I wanted to sleep the night away, but that never happened.

Every time my dreams started, my stomach lurched and woke me up. The night dragged on forever, and around five o'clock in the morning, I gave up and pulled out my laptop to watch some anime from under my covers.

I finished the first few episodes of a show called *Banana Fish* by the time the sun brightened my room enough to call it morning. I pulled on a pair of sweatpants and a T-shirt, avoiding the mirror on my way out the door.

Being the only person in the house, I felt like a giant walking down the stairs. Every creak seemed overly loud, and again, I didn't look into my parents' empty bedroom, not wanting to remind myself they were still gone.

The weird dog that Levi was, he usually slept most of the time. When he wanted to play, he chewed on a toy in a corner somewhere. We were more alike than I would have guessed. He got up and stretched his long body when I made it to the bottom of the stairs, wagging his tail happily. He leaned into my leg as I dug my fingers into his thick fur and rubbed behind his ears.

Even though my parents let me pick out his name, they never knew it came from one of my favorite anime series.

"Maybe I'll let you sleep with me tonight," I told the dog. He twitched an ear back toward the sound of my voice. "Just don't tell Mom, all right?"

Levi trotted to the kitchen ahead of me and I let him outside. A thin layer of frost covered the grass but the sun was bright with the coming morning. It was going to be a nice Saturday, even though I'd be stuck in the house sick all day.

I leaned against the counter, wondering if my stomach would handle food. I rarely got sick, but last night's episode put me on edge. I decided to wait it out and see. I kept thinking about Reid, wondering if I would see him again, wondering if I *wanted* to see him again.

My cell phone buzzed from my pocket, startling me out of my thoughts. I dug it out and saw that it was Mom. I sat down at the kitchen table and swiped to answer it.

"Hey, Mom."

"Hey, sweets. I didn't think you'd be up already, but I decided to try anyway," she said. "I didn't know you had anything going on this morning."

"No, I don't, I just couldn't sleep. My stomach decided to act up around midnight last night, so I stayed up."

"Your stomach? Do you think you're getting the flu?" I heard my dad's voice in the background, and I imagined Mom trying to shush him.

"No, I don't think it's the flu. It felt weird, but I think it's over," I said anyway, needing to reassure her before mom mode took over.

There was a pause on the other end. I could still hear the news in the background, which Dad was probably watching. I picked at the wooden table with my fingernail, waiting for her to respond. Her silence made me nervous.

"Are you sure you're feeling all right, now? Tell me the truth, Sam."

"Yeah, Mom. I'm fine, really." *I wasn't.*

"All right, but tell me if you get sick again. Promise?"

"I promise." There was a pause and I heard honking in the background, so I asked, "Where are you guys, anyway?"

"Oh, we're in San Francisco. We have to go, but I'll try to call again tomorrow. Love you."

"Love you, too."

I assumed that phone call would be the most exciting thing to happen to me that day. I stared at the table for another few moments, thinking and seeing nothing, too tired to even care.

A knock on the front door jerked me awake. I wasn't expecting anyone. Maybe Dad was getting something from UPS. I unlocked the door, expecting a mailman.

63

It wasn't a mailman.

It was Reid.

My hand froze on the handle, along with my whole body.

He half-heartedly smiled. "Hey."

The breeze brushed his dark hair, and his cheeks were slightly red from the cold air. One side of his jaw was bruised from the fight, and I spotted a cut above his eye. I should've stopped staring, but I couldn't.

After the immediate shock wore off, I quickly cleared my throat.

"Reid," I said, my brain finally catching up to what was happening. "What are you doing here?"

Did I mind that he was here? I still couldn't answer that—I hadn't had time to think about much of anything. Especially about what had happened the night before. Had I really last seen him only hours earlier?

"I'm sorry that I didn't"—he winced—"warn you I was coming or anything." He pulled his hand from one of his pockets, scratching the back of his head like it might be a nervous habit. "I just wanted to talk to you."

"About last night? Because I'm not sure if I want to talk about that . . ." I trailed off, reliving the memories of him fighting, and then the scene afterward. It seemed less scary now that we were standing in the sunshine, but last night had been dangerous and stupid.

"You don't want to talk about it at all, or not with me?"

His eyes pierced mine, and I didn't know what to say. My stomach tightened and I didn't want him to leave, but . . . something was *different* about him. Something within me wanted to know what it was.

"Last night was a lot to take in. You were in that fight and then—" I paused. He searched me as I struggled with my words. "And then I found you with that gang."

"They aren't a gang. I'm not into anything like that, I promise." Reid looked behind him, almost like he was worried they were going to be standing there in the street.

"Then who are they?"

"They're—" Reid shut his mouth like he was catching himself doing something he shouldn't. He averted his gaze.

I shook my head. "You came here to talk with me, but you're not going to?"

I didn't want to leave him standing on my doorstep. I didn't want to close the door in his face. And I also didn't want this to be the last time I saw him. But he wasn't telling me anything.

"Sam, please, it's just that I've never told anyone before." He let out a long breath, looking beaten. "I don't know *how*."

"Tell me *anything* then, so long as it's true."

I waited, but a long moment passed, and he didn't say a word.

"Fine." I shook my head, not wanting to do what I was doing. I closed the door and backed away from it, staring at the dark wood between us. I hated myself for it.

"Sam, wait," he pleaded, his voice muffled.

It took everything I had to hold back my tears. My chest heaved, but I didn't seem to be getting enough air. I backed up against the wall under the stairs, glancing at the door to my right. I wondered if he was still out there, and I was afraid that he wasn't.

"Sam?"

Gosh I love the sound of his voice.

I shouldn't love the sound of his voice.

I swallowed the lump in my throat. "What?"

"Yesterday morning you asked me about what I did," he said carefully.

"And you wouldn't tell me," I replied.

"No, but I'm wondering if I can show you?" I could hear the nervousness in his voice.

"What do you mean, 'show me?'"

There was a moment of silence, and I looked toward the door again.

"Do you remember the fight last night?" he asked.

I did all too well. "Yeah, of course, what about it?"

"Did you notice anything . . . *odd* about it?"

I let out a breath. "Reid, you're not making any sense. I don't *know* what I saw last night. You—" I looked away from the door. "You were really good in that fight, but you were almost *too* good."

"Let me show you. It's the only way for you to understand."

I hesitated, unsure.

"Okay." I nodded, even though he couldn't see.

"Stay right there, all right?"

"I thought you were going to show me." How was he going to do that with a door between us?

"I am going to show you, but you need to stay there." Another moment of silence passed before he said, "And, Sam, *please* don't freak out."

With those words, nerves settled into my stomach. I didn't know what to expect.

Then it happened.

The air rippled right before my eyes, like a thin veil of water. My heart pounded at the sight of it . . . and then Reid appeared. A slight breeze came with him, ruffling my hair, tickling my neck and cheeks. The fragile wisps of air that he came from slowly disappeared with his presence. They were like invisible strings in the wind, something I had never seen before. It was beautiful and frightening.

One second, Reid had been on the other side of the door, and now he was here, in the hallway of my house. He had just . . . *appeared*. He waited for my reaction, something that should have probably included running or screaming, but I did neither.

66

Was I dreaming again? I touched my stomach because I felt slightly sick and really started to doubt if any of this was real.

Reid caught on and asked, "Are you okay?"

"I'm not sure—am I dreaming right now?" I glanced around. Everything looked normal. Everything except Reid's appearing in front of me out of thin air.

Reid hesitated and said, "No, you aren't dreaming."

The wave of sickness passed, leaving me with nervousness, fear of the unknown, and a bit of curiosity.

"Reid, you—" I searched his eyes, as dark and warm as ever. He was nothing but real. "What did you do?"

He stepped closer, to the point where only a foot separated us. He smelled like the air, but the air you would find in the middle of a field in some unknown land. The way your hair smells after you have ridden a roller coaster or your skin after you have ridden a motorcycle.

"You didn't freak out." He studied me. "Why didn't you freak out?"

I shook my head slowly. "I don't know. Does everyone else freak out when you show them?"

"I've—never shown anyone before. You're the first."

His response puzzled me but also made me feel like maybe I actually meant something to him. Didn't he have any family or friends? Maybe he'd never told them.

"What *is* it exactly?" I felt stupid for asking, like I was asking him what a car was.

Reid gave me a crooked smile. "It's drifting."

"That guy last night, with the Australian accent, he mentioned drifters. I didn't know what it meant. I just thought it was gang slang. Is that what you are? A . . . drifter?" My breathing still came faster than normal, but I think it was just because he was close to me more than anything else.

"Yeah, and so is Jake, my friend."

"And what about those men last night? Are they drifters, too?"

His smile dropped as he scratched the back of his head again. "No, they're not, but they aren't normal either."

I tried to make sense of everything he said. It was nearly impossible. Reid was . . . different, and I thought I was okay with that. But I still didn't *know* anything about him. Where was he from? Did he have any siblings or family? How long had he had this ability and how did he get it? Was he born with it or was it more of a Peter Parker-type situation?

I had so many questions for him, and now that I knew this tiny piece of him, I needed to know more.

"I know it's a lot to take in," he said. "I'm sorry."

He waited for my response.

"Okay, yeah . . ."

"Okay?"

"I mean—" I threw up my hands and said, "I'm just still trying to process this. *Everything.* Everything is just so—"

"—Sam."

The room started to spin, and I felt for the wall behind me, needing something solid. Reid reached out for my wrist and said, "Just breathe."

"What?" I asked, practically breathless.

"Just . . . breathe. Don't worry about anything. It's you and me. We're in the hallway. It's nice and quiet."

Reid let the silence hang between us, and my heart slowed a bit, because he was right. It was just us here, and the questions about Reid were slowly pushed to the back of my mind, ready for when I really needed them. Because there was only one fact I cared about right now: Reid, holding my wrist, smelling like wind and rain.

He wasn't lying to me. I'd seen it happen with my own eyes. The truth settled inside me, calmer than before.

There was only one question I wanted an answer to right then.

I swallowed and asked, "Why did you come here?"

"Because I wanted to give you answers."

"No, why did you *really* come here? Why me?"

His jaw flexed, and I worried that I had asked the wrong thing. Because how could someone like Reid like someone like me? But instead of brushing off my question, Reid said, "This is the first time I've met someone I wanted to share my secret with. I don't want to walk away from that type of thing."

Oh.

He kept going. "Look, I know this is a lot to take in, so I'll come back later. I'll knock on your door. If you don't answer, I'll never bother you again, I promise. But if you do decide you want to see more of me"—he stepped closer and lowered his voice—"I'll show you things you'll never forget."

I could feel the warmth from his breath, and my heart raced even more. He was so close, it felt like we could kiss without moving.

"Close your eyes," he said.

The moment after I did, I felt a rush of air sweep across my face. When I opened my eyes, he was gone. I stayed in that spot for a few more minutes, trying to think through what had just happened.

I slid down the length of the wall, my legs too weak to hold me up. Then I swore, multiple times, and only the dog was there to witness it. A couple minutes later, I really did throw up. Whether it was from shock or being sick, I wasn't sure.

I just knew I wanted to see Reid again, no matter what that looked like.

REID

NEW YORK, UNITED STATES

IT WAS HARD LEAVING SAM. I HAD TO HOLD myself back from touching her and getting too close. But I'd been close enough to breathe her in. That was all I needed for my blood to race.

When I left her, I drifted into Manhattan, wanting somewhere to go without thinking about it. But as I stood there, staring at a pretzel stand, my stomach complaining, I knew I needed to go someplace entirely different to take my mind off things until later when I'd go back to Sam. I couldn't stand around all day wondering if she would want to see me again, if she'd answer when I knocked on the door. I wanted nothing more. I'd felt a thrill run through me when I showed her my ability—even more so when she didn't freak out about it. Everything could still change—there was a chance she wouldn't let me in when I returned—but there was hope, too. Hope that she'd open the door and let me into her life and that I'd finally be open and honest and wholly me.

My stomach rumbled, reminding me Buck took all my money. I thought about going back to my apartment only because I might've left food there. As I thought more about my bed, my eyes became heavier, and I remembered I hadn't slept much last night.

"Are you going to buy something, buddy?" a thick Brooklyn accent asked.

I blinked myself back to reality, seeing that the pretzel vendor stared back at me with an impatient expression on his face.

"Um, no."

"Well, would you mind moving then?" he asked rudely. "I don't think people would want to stop if there's some punk kid standing in the way."

I blinked and looked around, seeing nobody.

"What are you, high?" he asked again.

I sighed and decided to go home. But before I went, I said, "No, but I think you are."

An unfortunate side effect of drifting is that it's impossible to see their faces after I've disappeared in front of them. I would have loved to have seen his shocked expression and his mouth hanging open. I didn't do it often—rarely, actually, because of the number of cameras, cell phones, and possibly satellites spying on me from above. But sometimes I couldn't resist.

I drifted right into my room, because I still had secrets to keep. It was in an old condemned apartment building that could be torn down any day now, but somehow other kids had found a home in it, just as I had. I could hear them downstairs, fighting over something stupid. About a dozen lived here, all kids who had run away from foster homes or real homes where they didn't feel like they belonged anymore.

Old pictures from the previous owners still hung on the wall, and there was nothing but cabinets for a kitchen. But nothing looked cozier than my bed in the corner, placed right underneath the window.

I went over to the old dresser where I kept a few changes of clothes and a stash of food if I had any. It looked empty, but hidden in the corner was a bag of Cheetos. My mouth watered as I devoured them. I must have looked pathetic, standing in front of a dresser eating a single bag of chips. I knew I needed a shower, and I'm sure dark bags marked my eyes from my sleepless night.

After throwing the Cheetos bag in the trash, I dropped down on my bed. The light splattered over my body as I watched my stomach rise and fall. I needed more to eat. If I didn't eat, I couldn't fight, and if I couldn't fight, I wouldn't eat. It was a never-ending cycle.

I hated stealing food. Not as much as stealing money, but it still left a bad taste in my mouth. But sometimes I didn't have a choice.

I stood outside a supermarket somewhere in Madison, New Jersey. It was just past noon and business was picking up. Cars crowded the parking lot and an attendant was busy rounding up the shopping carts. The employees inside would be occupied with customers, and it's not like they would see me entering the store anyway.

I took a chance and drifted right into the stockroom. I appeared in the back corner, and there was nobody around. I waited a few moments to make sure and then opened my bag. I'd left everything at home so I could fit enough to last me though the weekend. I knew of a lower-class bar that held fights every Monday night. That's when I would get paid next.

I never made as much as the fight clubs. The *real* fight clubs.

With my bag full, I drifted to Jake's apartment since I knew he wouldn't be there. He was rarely in New York, and when he did come into town, he never stayed long. I was only going to be there long enough to take a shower.

Sometimes I would go to a gym's locker room; closed or not, it didn't matter. If people see you there, they just assume you have a membership. But locker rooms weren't as nice, or quiet, as Jake's apartment.

I dropped my bag on the couch and headed for the bathroom. I started the shower, watching the steam roll out of the top of the glass wall, about to cherish a wonderful moment.

Pulling off my shirt, I caught a glance of myself in the mirror. The bruises from last night were still fresh. I hadn't looked in a mirror for a long time, and my body was still in relatively good shape, but if I didn't start eating well—and often—again, I would start losing weight and muscle.

I'd been a small kid, and usually the shortest in my class, but throwing punches every few days made me just as strong as everyone else and I finally grew to a normal height. Unlike when I was younger, I could take care of myself now.

The hot water felt scalding against my cold skin, and I welcomed it. Showers were a luxury, and I didn't get to take them often enough. If I could have it my way, I would take one every day. I let the water run over my head for an extra five minutes, just because, the heat relaxing my sore muscles.

My thoughts drifted as I was under the hot water, and I thought of Sam and smiled. Whenever I was away from her, I wanted to see her again, and when I was with her, I wanted to be closer. But on the other hand, I was confused, because I never really knew what she was thinking or what she wanted. In many ways, we were still strangers, yet somehow I had trusted her with my deepest secret.

One thing was clear: I wanted to keep seeing her.

I took my time getting dressed and even used Jake's blow-dryer so I wouldn't catch a cold from having a wet head in this weather. I made myself a cup of coffee and enjoyed the view for a few minutes before getting ready to leave. I had a lot of time before tonight, and I thought of a few ways to pass the time—snowboarding somewhere in Europe or finding a lecture to sit in on at an Ivy League school instead of the community colleges I frequented. I didn't officially *go* to school, but I was still learning new things every week.

I pulled my jacket on, when there was a knock at the door. I instantly froze. Nobody knew Jake in the city, so I had no idea who it could be. I slowly crept toward the door and looked through the peephole. There were two men outside who looked a lot like detectives—judging from the badges hanging from their necks.

I quickly backed away when another knock came.

"NYPD, we just want to ask a few questions," a voice said from behind the door.

Why were the police at his door? I knew Jake got his money from stealing, but I didn't think he would ever get caught for it. I had to leave and find him—he needed to know that the police were looking for him. With my heart racing, I thought hard about Jake.

A picture formed in my mind: he stood outside of a café, talking to a pretty girl with dark hair. It was nighttime, and the restaurant lights were illuminated behind them. It was like a scene from a romantic movie.

Typical.

I didn't wait another moment and drifted into a nearby alley. The next thing I knew, I was breathing in the scent of the small southern town in France. People on the street didn't look twice as I stepped onto the sidewalk. The streets were busy with Saturday-night shoppers.

Jake faced my direction. As I got closer, his eyes flickered over to me, but he didn't react in any other way, still talking to the woman next to him as though I didn't exist. That in itself surprised me; I rarely came to see him, so I had expected more of a reaction.

"I need to talk to you," I said when I reached him.

Jake and the woman looked at me, like they weren't at all surprised to see me there. The woman was rather tall with dark skin and hair, wearing jeans and a thin blouse with a light jacket.

"I was actually about to come find you," Jake stated.

"You were? What for?"

He glanced around at the thick crowd surrounding us. "Let's take this someplace else, yeah?" Jake walked off toward the alleyway I'd come from, and to my surprise, the woman followed him. I had just thought she was a random date.

I followed the two of them down the narrow alley until we came up on a dead end.

"There were cops at your door just now," I said before I even stopped walking.

"Cops?" he asked, raising an eyebrow. "And why were you at my place?"

"Detectives, actually. And I was taking a shower." I shrugged.

He smiled. "Well, it looks like you won't be able to use it again either. Somebody probably gave them my name. Buck, no doubt, and he would do the same thing to you if you weren't homeless."

"That's beside the point."

"Yeah, well, just don't go back there. I'll find another flat soon."

"What about the cops?" He didn't seem worried about them at all, but of course, it wasn't like we could be locked up in a cell either.

Jake paused, looking at the woman beside him. She raised her eyebrow. "That's the least of my worries right now," he said.

"The least of your worries?" I asked, looking between them. "What's going on?"

"Reid, this is Sabrina. She's a friend of mine from Spain, and she just told me some interesting news."

"Sabrina." I nodded. "I've heard of you."

"You have?" she asked, her accent barely noticeable.

"No."

She smirked wickedly. "Well, I've heard of you, and you're shorter than I thought you'd be."

I heard Jake let out a quick breath in an attempt to suppress his laughter. When he caught sight of my face, he cleared his throat and said, "But seriously, Reid, this is something that concerns you, too."

"What is it?"

"There have been . . . drifters going missing."

"*Missing?*" I asked, because while we could disappear and often did, we didn't stay missing. Drifters didn't get lost, and the only people able to go up against us were sliders.

Sabrina cut in, like she was reading my thoughts. "Taken, actually. And we think Knox is behind it."

"What for?" I asked. "Do we know why?"

"Not yet," Sabrina said. "We aren't sure what his next move is going to be, so we're watching him and trying to get evidence, so we know for sure."

Then Jake said, "There's another meeting tonight. You should join us for once."

"And break my perfect record of absent attendance?" I asked with a grin. "I'll pass. Besides, I have plans. But keep me posted if it gets serious."

Even though I was acting as if the news didn't bother me, it really did. Buck already had it out for me, and since he was working for Knox, what if he decided I needed to be next?

I kept up my facade, not wanting Jake to become overprotective.

76

He said, "*Plans?* Reid, you never have plans."

"Well, I do tonight."

"Fine, but be careful, all right? I'll come find you later, hopefully with a new apartment."

I nodded. "Fine."

They left me in a city I had no desire to be in with a lot of hours to kill before tonight.

So I decided to see if my one other friend wanted to grab brunch somewhere.

I drifted outside of his house on Long Island and picked my way through the bushes until I got a view of the back of the house. From across the pool and the plush lounge chairs, I spotted Gavin sitting at the breakfast table with his sister and mother, a plate of untouched food in front of him as they talked about something he clearly didn't care about.

I moved to the left a bit, so I had a better angle on him without his family seeing, and then I waved my arms. His eyes shifted, spotting me, and he tried to hold back from smiling. Gavin excused himself from the table, and being the good boy that he was, he took some dirty dishes to the sink before stepping out the back door.

He met me on the other side of the bushes. "I'm thinking the only time you come see me is when you're hungry."

"That's not—" I couldn't even be bothered to lie. "Okay, maybe, but it's our *thing.*"

The first time we met was in a grocery store in Philadelphia. His family was in town that week visiting relatives, so it was totally random seeing him in a store in the middle of the night. He stole for the rush of it, and I needed to eat, and we both saw each other for what we were—a slider and a drifter who didn't care about the feud that was supposed to keep us apart.

We hung out in the store until the employees started to show up in the morning, eating Swiss Rolls and Cheetos, talking about everything from school to families to what we liked to do in our free time.

From then on, I always showed up to visit him at random times and places, and he always made an excuse to go somewhere with me.

I had needed a friend more than anything back then, and Jake was always more like a brother. Gavin and I were just good together and I liked his company.

The one thing we never talked about was our abilities. We knew what the other could do, but by not talking about it, the trust between us grew. It was an unspoken rule not to mention them, because our differences were supposed to keep us enemies.

So now, standing across from Gavin in his backyard, he couldn't say no.

He smiled and asked, "Where do you want to go?"

"Are you buying?"

"I can, but my wallet is upstairs."

I thought of the perfect place, which didn't require his wallet. I stashed my bag under the hedge and then took off my jacket. Without even warning him, I grabbed Gavin's hand and drifted us into a room with dozens of busy tables with families and kids running around. There was a huge buffet table with mounds of food and Gavin took in the situation.

"Where—"

That's when a loud, low-pitched horn echoed in from outside. It was unmistakably a boat horn, and Gavin put the pieces together.

"You brought us to a cruise ship?"

I shrugged. "The food is free."

Gavin gave me a look that said, *Can't argue with that*, and went to grab himself a plate. After we were full, we went up top and walked around the deck. The sun was hot and warm on my back, and we leaned against a railing, watching the water below.

"Remember that time we went to Denver to go snowboarding?" Gavin asked.

"Yeah, the day you almost ran into that tree?"

He smiled. "We don't talk about that." Then his smile slowly left and he said, "My dad mentioned going to that resort this winter, and I almost slipped up and told him how good it was." He was quiet for a moment and then glanced at me. "He thinks I've never been to Colorado before, and I almost spilled one of my biggest secrets."

What he didn't say was, *I* was the secret. In this world, we weren't supposed to be friends. Friendly, maybe, on a good day. But friends? Never.

Gavin said, "I just wish we didn't have to hide."

I almost replied with, *What's stopped you?* But I knew what it was. His family. I had nothing to lose by being his friend, but he could lose everything. His dad might even disown him, and he might've been kicked out of his house—anything could happen. Gavin once said there was a wall between him and his family, something he didn't think would ever come down.

The only family member he ever spoke fondly of was his grandmother who still lived in Pakistan. He saw her every year for Christmas, and he always came back in a better mood. Even though I'd never met her, I liked her because she made him happy.

I thought about the meeting happening right now, with Jake and the other drifters, and wondered if anything could ever happen that would push Gavin and me apart.

I hoped not.

I took Gavin back to his house an hour later in case his family started wondering where he was. Before he walked through the door, he turned and waved, telling me in one gesture that he still wanted to be my friend. No matter what.

Back at my apartment, I stashed my bags and pulled my fingers through my hair in an attempt to make it look good.

I couldn't wait any longer to see Sam.

I don't know if I can do this.

I'd never felt so nervous about anything before. I was more nervous now than I'd been that morning when I exposed my ability to her. My hands were almost to the point of shaking. I had to get it over with.

I took a deep, nervous breath and drifted to the sidewalk outside her house. The street was almost dark that fall evening, and the only light came from the street lamps overhead. I looked up at Sam's house, took a deep breath, then went up to her door.

I paused on the top step for a moment, then knocked. It was quiet inside, and every second she didn't open the door, my hope sank. It felt like an eternity.

Still nothing.

I backed down to the bottom step with my stomach aching, feeling defeated. She didn't want to see me again. I felt a strange panic rise within me, which never happened. I kept staring at the door, though, wishing she would still open it.

That's when I heard the lock turn.

SAM

NEW YORK, UNITED STATES

TODAY WAS THE SLOWEST DAY OF MY LIFE. I DIDN'T know what to do with myself. I ended up going to the park with Levi around noon and then took the long way home, needing more fresh air.

But then I was back in the house in the afternoon with nothing else to do. I thought about starting another puzzle, and then I thought about watching a movie. Neither seemed quite right—I had too much buzzing energy to sit still.

It didn't help that a headache had burrowed deep and didn't intend on leaving anytime soon. All day long, random images bombarded my mind until I thought about something else really hard. A quiet beach somewhere, a busy street in London, and of course, my thoughts always went back to the cliffs next to the ocean. The only thing that took my mind off of my headache and weird images was Reid.

Even thinking about him made me smile. *How can I not see him again?* There were reasons, of course. He was a stranger, for one, and I knew near nothing about him or anything about his past. But nothing felt *wrong* about him. Everything felt *right*.

He made me feel seen. He made me feel wanted.

Oh yeah, and he had a *superpower*.

I wasn't sure when Reid would come back, so I made sure to have decent clothes on. I probably changed outfits at least three times, which was unlike me, and I even brushed my hair.

The knock came in the evening, after dark. I was upstairs when I heard it and didn't even hesitate. I hurried down the steps, worried that I was taking too long and he would be gone by the time I reached the door.

Instead, I was greeted by his smile, and my heart pounded so hard that I could only manage to smile back.

"For a minute, I thought you weren't going to come," he said.

"Thought it would be more suspenseful this way," I joked. Then after a pause, I said, "I'm sorry, I was upstairs."

"Don't be. You're here." Then he asked, "Would you like to go somewhere with me?"

"Like—a date?" My voice was so high-pitched it was embarrassing.

Luckily, Reid didn't seem to notice.

"If you want to call it that. Or we could just call it hanging out?" he suggested.

He nodded for me to join him on the sidewalk. A thrill of unexpectedness ran through my veins, and the night didn't seem so cold anymore. I was nervous about going with him and where he would take me, but I wanted nothing more.

I joined him outside after slipping on my shoes, and after that, I didn't know what to do. Being alone on a quiet street, with a boy I barely knew, was oddly exhilarating.

"Where are we going?" I asked.

He looked around the street, his eyes glinting under the streetlights. The night was cold, and our breath could be seen white in the air. Reid looked back at me and my stomach stirred. It was a foreign feeling. I wanted more of it.

"Take my hand." His words were strong and so confident. He gave me a crooked smile to wipe away any insecurities I might've had.

Reid's hand was warm around mine, and every nerve ending was on fire.

"Don't let go, all right?" I nodded and was almost afraid for what was about to happen. "And you might want to close your eyes for the first time, just to be safe."

I stepped closer to him and closed my eyes, holding his hand like it was my lifeline.

We took a single step forward and then it felt like we were free-falling. My stomach turned and there was nothing but air under my feet. Wisps of hair brushed across my forehead and then I was on solid ground again. It was over. Not even a second had passed.

"Sam."

"What?"

"You can open your eyes now," he whispered.

I still didn't, afraid of what I might see. Even though I kept my eyes closed, I knew we weren't in the city anymore. The car sounds were replaced with just the wind and the sway of blowing grass.

I cracked my eyes open and all I saw was green grass and bright sunlight. It took a moment for my eyes to adjust, and then all I could do was stare. The grass, the large tree a little to the left, and then the field that stretched around us. The air was so *warm* and the sky was so blue.

"How do you feel? Are you nauseated at all? Dizzy? Panicked?"

I took my stomach into consideration. It had felt queasy all day, but right now, it felt like I'd never been sick.

"I'm fine . . . more than fine." I glanced at him. "Where are we?"

He didn't let go of my hand, but instead walked forward and tugged me along. I followed behind toward the lone tree in the sea of grass. Its branches spread far across the ground, shading the ground they covered.

Reid let go of my hand and smiled. "We're not in Kansas anymore."

I nodded, still trying to get my bearings. "We aren't?"

I'm not sure how I was so calm on the outside, because on the inside, I was swearing up a storm. It wasn't just my imagination or some prank; he was serious. It was real. He was telling the truth. *How, how, how?*

"Is this real?" I voiced, not even meaning to say it aloud.

Reid nodded and said, "Come on, I want to show you something."

SAM

TANGOIO, NEW ZEALAND

REID STARTED OFF AND I FOLLOWED HIM through the field. Soon I picked up the sound of waves. We came to the top of a small hill, and as far as I could see was blue water and clear skies.

"Are you going to tell me where we are yet?"

"New Zealand."

"Seriously?" I asked, turning to him.

He nodded, smiling. "Yeah, why not?"

"I mean . . . if I was going to choose New Zealand, I would at least go to the places where they made *The Lord of the Rings*, like any other normal human, obviously."

"Yeah, the mountains are nice, sure," Reid admitted, because of course he'd already seen them. "But I like this place, too. It's . . . peaceful."

Reid sat down in the grass and I joined him, still taking in the view.

"When did you learn you could do it?" I asked. "Or could you always?"

"No, I was eight when I drifted for the first time. It's

different for everyone, though. Some don't figure out they can until they're older."

Listening to him talk about himself, and other people like him, made me feel like he was part of some alien species. I found myself wanting to know everything about him, but I was afraid he would disappear before I found out everything.

"You said I was the first person that you've ever shown your drifting to. Is that true?"

"Yeah, my friends have always known, but you're the first person I've ever *told*. Like the first 'outsider.'"

"What about your parents? Do they know?"

Reid's dark eyes glanced away from mine and I instantly knew I shouldn't have asked. "They did, yeah." He shook his head and shrugged his shoulders, like it was hard using the past tense when talking about them.

I wished I hadn't asked and wondered if I should apologize. But saying I was sorry didn't seem like enough.

Instead, I asked, "Do you have any brothers or sisters?"

"No, it's just me."

I nodded, letting it go.

"What about you?" he asked after a little while.

"I have an older brother. He's away at college, though."

"I've always kinda wished I'd had an older brother, or any sibling really." He shrugged again. "I guess Jake is the closest thing I've come to one."

"How long have you known him?"

"I think it's been about five years now, but it seems longer. I don't see him that often. Just when he comes into town to see if I'm staying out of trouble." He smiled to himself. He opened his mouth as if he were about to say something more, then decided against it.

I didn't press him. I was already grateful he was talking at all. It seemed like he was usually just as quiet as I was, so I understood not wanting to talk about certain things at certain times.

"What about those guys at the club last night? You said they were—"

"Different?" he finished for me, smiling crookedly. His dimple appeared again. "That one is a little harder to explain, but I'll try. They are different like us, but they're called *sliders*. Instead of drifting, they have the ability to manipulate time around themselves."

I knew my eyes must have widened, because he smiled at my reaction.

"So what does that mean?" I asked, still bewildered by the possibility.

"To the naked eye, it would look like they were moving really fast. You know Quicksilver from *X-Men*? It's like that. But even they have boundaries. They can only do it for a certain amount of time, and it's usually just short bursts of it."

"Why can't they do it for longer?"

"Both of our abilities are similar in their opposites. Both have limits. It's the curse that comes with the power."

"So if the sliders can't manipulate time forever, what can't you do?"

He seemed to wince slightly. "It's more of a question of what we *don't* do. Drifting is a part of who we are, same as them. Except slowing time drains away their energy. If they keep doing it long enough, they'll die. But for us, it's the opposite." He looked toward the ground again, and when he looked up, he said, "If we don't drift, we die."

The silence in the air was thick. Reid's eyes were staring hard into mine, showing nothing but the truth. They were frighteningly real to look into.

"How long can you go without drifting?"

"A day without any side effects. After that, it gets worse.

The first couple of days I'd feel like I had the flu—aches, nausea, chills, restlessness, fatigue. Then after that, the hallucinations would come. I'd start seeing other places, like my body and mind were trying to force me to drift in order to save itself. It's like losing a vital organ. The longer you wait, the worse it gets."

A small shiver ran down my spine at his description of it. I wondered what it would be like to have to drift the rest of my life. I smiled because I didn't think it would be so bad, but why would anyone *stop* in the first place? That's what puzzled me.

After a moment, I gained enough courage to ask, "Why would that ever happen?"

"Like anyone else, we have our enemies."

The way he said it wiped the smile from my face. "Has it ever happened to you?"

Reid shook his head. "No, but there are stories. Years back, there were a few drifters who thought they were above any law and kinda went off the rails. A few other drifters took matters into their own hands and stopped them. Let's just say, it wasn't a good ending for them."

"Oh." I nodded because I didn't know what else to do.

We sat in silence for another few minutes before Reid winced and asked, "You want to go back?"

"Back home, or back to New York?"

He grinned and stood up, pulling me with him. "You tell me. You can still run away screaming if you'd like."

I shrugged one shoulder. "I'll pass, thanks. I'm sticking around until you take me to where *Harry Potter* was filmed since you so very disappointingly brought me to New Zealand and didn't even have the common decency to take me to Mordor."

"I'll never live that down, will I?"

"Only if you never take me."

Reid smiled like he was trying not to. "So, where do you want to go?"

"Let's go back to New York. This whole daytime when it's supposed to be nighttime thing is weird. But take me somewhere besides home. Take me somewhere you love in the city."

Reid nodded, happy to oblige, and held out his hand. "This time keep your eyes open, if you want."

I could only nod from the anticipation coiling in my stomach. I took his hand and stood closer to him, breathing in the air and his scent, which seemed to be the same.

When we stepped forward, the air rippled around us, like smoke running over glass, thin and wispy. Day turned to night in an instant as the world changed. It felt as if I was free-falling again, and yet we weren't. We stood on ground that wasn't there, until the world became clear once more and we were somewhere else entirely.

I felt like I couldn't breathe until my feet were on solid ground again, but maybe it was just me holding my breath. It was like going down the big hill of a roller coaster—however many times you ride it, your stomach always drops.

The roof we appeared on looked over Central Park, the bright buildings of New York outlining the blackened sections of trees in the center of the busy city. Paths were illuminated by pale lights, making a maze through the dark park.

We were so far up that the loud sounds of the street below were almost to the point of being muted. It was like a hideaway where nobody could see or hear.

"Are we near Fifth Avenue?" I asked.

"Yeah, it's right below us."

Reid led me to the edge before releasing my hand. We looked over, down to the streets below, with the slight breeze pushing our hair around. The temperature had dropped more, and the change in temperature made me shiver. The sunshine in New Zealand had been nice.

"Are you cold?"

"A little."

"Sit by me?"

Even though it was a question, the want in his voice was unmistakable.

I followed him to the other edge and watched as he sat down on the parapet, letting his legs hang over. I'd never had a problem with heights, so I joined him on the ledge without a second thought. When I was seated, Reid moved closer to me, so our legs and arms were brushing against each other.

"Is that better?"

I felt his eyes on me, but I didn't look at him, afraid he would see my reddening cheeks. I nodded, keeping my eyes on the park below. I watched the people, but the only person I could think about was the boy next to me. But what I didn't get was, why me? Why had Reid decided to show himself to *me*?

"Reid . . ." From my peripheral vision, I saw him look at me. "Why me? I mean, why did you even talk to me that day on the subway?" I stared at my shoes as they dangled in the air, hundreds of feet over the street. I was nervous for his answer, like he would suddenly realize his mistake and change his mind.

"Other than the fact I think you're cute?"

I smiled and nudged him in the shoulder. "I'm serious, I want to know."

He grinned, his dark eyes somehow bright in the night. "I *am* serious."

"There has to be another reason."

He hesitated. "There is, but . . ."

"Tell me."

Reid scratched the back of his head and avoided my gaze.

"Because you noticed me before you knew about my ability. You noticed me even when you thought I was normal, before you ever got to know me. That's why I knew you were special."

Special. That was one word that nobody had ever used to describe me before.

I stared at him even after he looked away, down to the street and people below. I found myself not wanting to be anywhere else in the world than right where I was at that moment.

REID

NEW YORK, UNITED STATES

SAM WAS QUIET FOR A LONG TIME AFTER I ADMIT-ted some things I probably shouldn't have. Her eyes stared downward, not focused on anything particular. I wanted to somehow change the subject but didn't know how.

"You've been quiet for a long time, you know," I said.

Her eyes finally moved, but she still stared down at the street. "Sorry, I was thinking."

"About what?"

"Stuff like how everyone makes the mistake of not noticing you," she answered.

When she turned to look at me, a smile tugged at her lips. I held her gaze until it started to become awkward, and then I said, "Well, I'm glad you didn't make the same mistake." We stared out over the park for a few minutes in silence. I peeked over at her and she stole a glance, smiling again. "So did I ruin your Saturday night plans?"

Sam laughed once to herself and shook her head. "I never have plans. Once in a while my friend, Nella, will make me go

92

somewhere with her—like last night—but I usually stay in and watch anime or something."

When she said *last night*, I had to stop and think about it. *It really was just last night.* It seemed like a week ago.

"Actually," she started, "can I ask you something about that? I know I still don't know much of anything, but why do you fight at the clubs?"

I was afraid this question would lead to other unwanted subjects. Subjects I wasn't ready to touch yet. I knew telling her was eventually the right thing to do, especially if I wanted to keep seeing her, but I was still hesitant. My past and personal life was something I kept to myself. The only person who truly knew me was Jake.

But I wanted Sam to know me, too.

I decided to tell her the truth, but only as much as I could bear. One truth at a time.

"It's good money, and I like the quick cash." *And I do it because I need to eat.* That was the whole truth, but only half of it made its way out of my mouth.

"How often do you do it?"

"As often as I can without being noticed. It wouldn't do me any good to be recognized as the guy who always wins."

"How did you do that, by the way, without it being visible to everyone else?"

"The action is small, and so is the drift. In a way, it's almost invisible. It just appears like I'm moving fast and people believe it, because in their eyes, what other explanation is there?"

I nodded, thinking about that fight again. "Is that why the sliders were after you last night? Because you always win?"

"Yeah, pretty much. Buck would like nothing more than to drive me out of town."

"So you live here then? In the city, I mean."

I swallowed and found my mouth dry. I wasn't sure why I thought I could pull off not telling her—of course I had to. It was easier showing her things rather than trying to explain it all. I'd never been great with words. But could I do that with other things, too?

I said, "I'm sorry that I've been hesitant. I've never told anyone this stuff before and it's a lot. For both of us. It's hard for me to explain everything at once."

She half smiled. "Is that why you *showed* me this morning, instead of just telling me?"

I cringed a little at remembering her shocked face. "*Yeahhh.*" I let the word drag out.

"Does this mean you're going to show me something else?"

"If you want me to," I answered hesitantly. I was nervous about showing her where I lived, but it was the only way to show her who I truly was. It wasn't something I could hide from. "I want to tell you beforehand that I might not be who you think I am. Apart from drifting, my life isn't all that great."

I averted my eyes from hers, afraid of seeing something I didn't want to. I swung my legs back around onto the roof without waiting for an answer. Sam followed me and silently stepped up to my side to grasp my hand. I loved the feeling of hers in mine.

"I still don't think it'll change anything," she said.

I looked over at her. "I hope it doesn't."

I felt her hand tighten around mine as I drifted. My room was immersed in blackness from the night and lack of street lamps outside. The only people who came around this area usually didn't care about having good lighting; in fact, they usually relied on it being the opposite.

"Nice place."

I smiled at the sarcasm in her voice. "Hold on, let me find a light."

"When you turn it on, am I going to find dead bodies hanging from the ceiling or something?" She laughed nervously.

I let out a low chuckle. "No, nothing like that." I let go of her hand and made my way blindly to the battery-powered lamp near my bed. I turned the knob, illuminating the small room in a dull glow. I stood and looked at Sam. She wasn't looking at me, just everything around me, taking me in in my natural environment. There wasn't much to look at.

Her eyes traveled over the nonexistent kitchen and lone dresser, and to my pathetic bed that didn't even have a box spring or frame, and then finally to me. I didn't know what to do with myself. I felt awkward standing there as she realized I was practically homeless.

Why did I even bring her here? Would it have been better if I'd lied to her and brought her to someone else's apartment while they were gone? Pretended Jake's place was mine instead?

I stopped thinking, knowing the moment had already passed. I'd made my decision. It was up to Sam now whether she still wanted to be around me.

"I'm sorry I'm nothing more than this," I said.

"I never asked for anything more."

I couldn't tell if she was lying, but I wanted to believe the sincerity in her words.

"Then what do you want, Sam?" I asked, my voice weak. "Because I don't have anything except this. It's just me. You can't possibly want that."

A lump formed in my throat as I thought about my life, knowing it amounted to nothing. How could she not see that I wasn't worth it?

Nobody, nobody, nobody.

"Reid?"

I blinked, bringing myself out of my thoughts and back

95

to her eyes. "Tell me the truth," I whispered. "Am I who you thought I'd be?"

She shook her head. "No, not in the slightest." But before I could respond, she stepped closer to me, a little less than a foot away. "You're so much more. It sounds really corny to say it out loud, but it's true."

I opened my mouth to speak, hesitant at first. "But I'm not. This is all I am. How can you say that I'm more?"

"It's not about what you have or what you don't have. I've already seen enough to know that you're different from everyone else, but for the better, and not just because of your drifting."

"But you barely know me."

"That's why I'm here, right?"

We stared at each other, and I honestly thought it was because neither of us knew what to say. *I* sure didn't.

Her phone made some noise from her pocket and she broke eye contact, pulling it out. I looked away. A small sigh came from her, and I glanced to see her texting someone.

"It's my friend, Nella. She's wondering what I'm doing because she's bored. There's no doubt she's on her way to my house right now."

"Do you want to go back?"

"No, but I probably should." She winced. "I haven't told her anything about you. She'll probably freak out if I'm not there when she shows up."

"All right, I'll take you back." My voice sounded dull, but I tried not to give away that I didn't want her to leave. Sam nodded and held my hand again.

"I'm sorry," she mumbled.

I narrowed my eyes even though she wasn't looking at me. "What for?"

She shook her head. "Never mind. And you can take me

right inside. I don't want to appear on my doorstep if she's already there."

"Okay."

I thought of the hallway in her home and then we were there. It was dim, the only light coming from above the door, and it cast long shadows where we stood. It felt awkward between us; I was still turning our previous conversation over in my head, knowing how there were still so many questions and things left unsaid. How I wasn't sure I believed what she saw in me. I slowly stepped away from her and dropped her hand.

"I don't care if you think I'm wrong, but I know what's right," Sam said, almost like she'd been reading my thoughts. When I didn't respond, she asked, her voice quieter, "Why do you live there? Where's your family?"

The very question I was trying to avoid. I pushed my hands into my pockets. I opened my mouth, trying to find the words.

"My parents died a few years ago," I started, not knowing how else to say it. "I didn't have any other family." I shifted my weight, feeling her eyes on me. "A police officer drove me to the station and I sat there for a really long time until a lady came to talk to me. She was trying to find a temporary home for me to stay in until they could find somewhere permanent."

I paused, not sure if I should keep going. Sam's eyes were unwavering, waiting for me to tell the rest.

"After the woman said *permanent*, I couldn't stop thinking about that word and how wrong it was. Permanent was supposed to mean living at home with my parents. I didn't want a new family because I already had one. The woman left me for a little while and I stared at the pictures framed on the desk and I did the only thing I knew. I just—I just *left*." I took a deep breath and finished with, "And I never went back."

Sam's skin looked pale in the light and her eyes were dark and wide, standing out. Then her shoulders relaxed a little, letting me breathe.

"I'm sorry you had to go through that."

"Don't be. I don't regret it." I decided it was time to change the subject.

"Can I tell you a secret about me?" she asked. "Seems only fair for me to share one now, too."

I nodded and she took a step forward, bringing her face alongside mine, her mouth next to my ear. Then she whispered, "I like you."

I was one hundred percent sure she could hear my thoughts screaming through me. *She likes me.* "You do?"

She pulled away, nodding. "Yes."

I wanted to kiss her more than anything. Just as I was thinking about trying to, a knock sounded from the front door. We quickly stepped away from each other, like we were guilty for being caught even though the person outside the door couldn't see us. I looked down the hall.

"That's probably Nella," she said.

"I'd better go."

"Reid, wait." She paused. "When will I see you next?"

"When do you want to see me?"

Another knock came and Sam cringed. "Soon." She nodded to herself. "Really soon. Please?"

I smiled. "Soon," I agreed.

I drifted with her smile etched into my mind, back into my room with the smell of crumbling cement in the air. I was still smiling as I slipped off my shoes and climbed into bed. I didn't bother taking off my clothes—it was warmer in the winter when I didn't. I flipped the light off and turned over to look out the window, watching the clouds pass over the moon. Finally, after what seemed forever, my eyes became heavy enough for sleep.

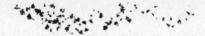

Sometime in the limbo between being asleep and awake, I heard someone drift into my room, disturbing the silence. The faint sound of a rushing breeze was soft but unforgettable. A hand grasped my shoulder and I swung out my elbow and hit him in the jaw.

"Hell, Reid, it's just me!" Jake backed away clutching his mouth. "I wasn't trying to kill you."

"What are you doing, sneaking in here like that?" I asked, still rattled.

I sat up against the wall and turned the light on. Jake grinned while he rubbed his jaw.

"What are you smiling about?" I asked.

"You just got back," he said, almost knowingly.

I raised an eyebrow as he sat on the end of my bed. Now that he was closer, he smelled like secondhand smoke and fresh air. Two smells that aren't normally found together.

"Yeah, so?"

"You hooked up with that girl, didn't you?"

"I didn't *hook up* with her." I smiled a bit and nodded. "But I was with her tonight."

"That's good. Are you going to see her again?"

"Yeah, probably tomorrow." My stomach fluttered at the prospect.

"And she didn't freak out when you told her?"

"Well, I didn't exactly tell her. I showed her because I didn't know how to explain it."

He laughed. "I can't believe the things you do sometimes." After I didn't say anything in response, he dropped his smile and said, "We still aren't sure who's taking drifters, but we have some people watching Knox." He eyed me. "You need to be careful."

"I am being careful—I haven't seen a slider in days."

Besides Gavin, but Jake didn't know about him, and I trusted Gavin so he wasn't worth mentioning.

He stood. "I'll let you sleep. I probably shouldn't come while you are passed out. Would have been safer for my jaw."

"Probably."

"I'll be getting another place tomorrow here in the city. I'll let you know where." I nodded as he backed away. "See you, mate." Jake had a knack for small talk, but sometimes I wished he wouldn't rush off so fast.

I sat against the wall for another few minutes, thinking about the tension between the drifters and sliders and wondered how it ever got to be so bad. We were different, so what? Now Knox might be making drifters disappear? Why?

We have always been at odds with each other, but now it seemed to be something deeper than what I could see on the surface.

I turned off the light and slipped under my covers again. Sleep was slow to come the second time, and the cold temperature wasn't helping. Winter came early this year, and my sleeping bag wasn't warm enough at below-freezing temperatures. In the winter, I would usually spend my nights somewhere in Florida, or even Arizona, but lately, I didn't feel like leaving the city.

For the first time in a long time, it felt like home.

SAM

NEW YORK, UNITED STATES

THE NIGHT HADN'T BEEN KIND. I DREAMED ABOUT the cliffs and ocean again, just as I'd imagined before getting on the train earlier that week. Except this time, the sky was starting to turn into day, and the grass was no longer frosted. My stomach was in a knot every time I woke up.

After exhaustion finally caught up with me, I slept a few hours straight until the sun woke me. I lay in bed for a good twenty minutes, trying to think about what was wrong with my stomach recently.

The easy answer would be the flu. It *was* flu season after all, and all of the symptoms pointed to it—well, besides the hallucinations. But deep down, I knew it wasn't the flu. It was something different. Something that scared me more than I liked to admit.

By the time I got showered and dressed, I felt more normal. My skin was still pale and there were bags underneath my eyes, but I saw no other evidence of my recent long nights. I pulled on a light sweatshirt and started downstairs. The way the house was quiet and the sun still rising reminded me of the previous morning when Reid had showed up so unexpectedly.

I wouldn't have minded if it happened again.

When I got to the bottom floor, Levi wasn't in his usual spot waiting for me.

"Levi?"

I waited to hear the rattling of his metal tags, but it never came. I knew I hadn't left him outside all night. I walked toward the kitchen in search of him.

There was movement outside and I saw Levi—someone was with him. At first, I thought he was attacking an intruder, but as I rushed to the door, I realized he was playing with the person. He was playing with Reid.

Reid had his arms out wide and was half-crouched, getting Levi all riled up. Reid's hair was crazy, like he'd been caught in a bad wind, and one of his shoes was untied. I smiled at the sight.

I stepped outside and Levi ran toward me. Reid straightened, giving me a smile in return.

"Hey," I said, petting Levi.

"Hey. Sorry if this is weird. I was waiting on your patio and your dog looked like he wanted to come out."

"No, it's fine. You're just here . . . *early*," I said.

"You said soon, didn't you?" He tried another smile, like he wasn't sure if he should.

"Well, yeah, but it's like . . ." I said, narrowing my eyes, "*early*, early."

Reid's smile slowly disappeared. "Sorry, was this not okay? Do you want me to go?"

"No." I shook my head. "I don't want you to go. Come inside."

"Are you feeling all right?" he asked, walking past me through the door. "You don't look so good."

"Oh, I've had a couple of rough nights. My stomach has been acting up lately. I think I might be getting the flu."

His shoulders lowered, and he asked, "So I'll take it you don't want to go anywhere today?"

I did, more than anything, but I knew I shouldn't. "I don't think that's a good idea."

"Yeah, probably not." Reid glanced around the room, looking like he was unsure he should be there.

"Stay here with me. We can watch a movie or something." I smiled as I thought of another idea. "You can even make me soup to help me feel better."

He lit up, happy he had a reason to stay. "I would love to."

Within the next hour, we both sat on the couch watching (me rewatching) the first couple episodes of *Stranger Things* because Reid had never seen it, and a piece of toast had safely settled in my stomach. Reid lounged next to me, wearing a black T-shirt that fit his upper body all too perfectly. I still couldn't believe he had agreed to stay with me. He could go anywhere in the world, and yet he was here with me on my couch watching TV.

"Do you want more toast?"

I shook my head. "I think that's enough for now."

"All right." He rose from the couch, taking my plate with him, and disappeared into the kitchen. I heard the faucet turn on. Then I realized he was actually washing my plate.

"You don't have to do that," I called.

"I know, but it's been a while since I've washed dishes." After a pause, he said quietly—like he wasn't sure he wanted to say it aloud—"It makes me feel normal."

I thought about where Reid lived and what the last few years must have been like for him, and I got an ache in my stomach. It wasn't a sickness ache; it was a longing. A lingering emotion that I had about him. It was a strange feeling.

Someone knocked on the door, and this time I knew it wasn't Reid. *Because he's in my house.* I smiled at the thought as I got up. When I opened the door, Nella greeted me with a grin.

"Let's watch movies," she said. "I'm done with homework, and I have nothing else to do."

"Oh, well . . ." I hesitated and didn't know how to respond. I glanced over my shoulder quickly, seeing if Reid was still in the kitchen.

Nella narrowed her eyes, knowing something was up. "What's going on? You're acting weird."

"It's nothing. I just haven't been feeling well."

"Well, do you want to watch a movie?"

I hesitated again and she caught on.

"*Sam*, what's going on? You're acting like there's a boy in there somewhere that you don't want me to find out about." When I didn't come up with a snarky comeback fast enough, her eyes grew wide. "Oh, my *gosh*, there's a boy in there and you didn't want me to find out."

I couldn't lie to her.

"Maybe?" I winced for the coming wrath. Before she could open her mouth, the door opened wider and Reid appeared beside me. Nella's eyes somehow opened even more at the sight of him.

"Nella, this is Reid."

She stared numbly at him as he shook her hand.

"It's nice to meet you," he said.

"Yeah—" Her eyes traveled back to mine, and I tried to give her a smile. She would drill me later, and by the look in her eyes, it wasn't going to be a good conversation, either. "So . . . I guess I'll see you later?"

"Yeah, did you want to meet up after school?"

"That's fine." Her eyes flickered to Reid, like she still couldn't believe he was standing there. Then she nodded once before leaving in an awkward silence. She was probably screaming inside; her responses were too simple and every one of them was left hanging. Very unlike Nella.

I watched her car pull away. The sky had become overcast with heavy clouds at some point, and I could hear the faint sound of thunder over the city noise.

"When do your parents get home?" Reid asked, his voice so close that it made me shiver—and not from the cold.

"They said it would be Tuesday." I shut the door, blocking out the late fall air. "Why?"

Reid shrugged and scratched the back of his head. "I don't know. Being here without them knowing kind of makes it feel like I'm doing something wrong."

"Oh." That was all I could say, half because it was true and half because I didn't want him to go. My parents had never set any house rules, probably because I'd never brought anyone home before.

"Do you want me to go?" he asked quietly.

"No."

"Then what should we do?"

I thought of something that would solve both problems. "Take me somewhere."

"But you're sick. Shouldn't you stay home?"

"I don't care," I said, shaking my head. "I don't want to spend the day inside, especially if it's going to rain and you're not going to be here."

He thought about it.

I asked, "Did you already have plans today?" I waited for his answer, holding my breath.

Reid looked up and laughed once. "No, I don't have plans. I was thinking about where we should go."

I smiled, unable to contain my excitement. "You think on that while I get ready."

I made sure Levi had food and water and then I disappeared upstairs for a few minutes to change into something more appropriate than my old sweatpants and T-shirt. Just when I was ready, I heard Reid talking to someone downstairs.

The voices were muffled, and when I got to the bottom floor, I saw that he was talking to his friend, Jake, in the kitchen. I didn't remember what he looked like, but his accent was hard to miss. I stopped at the bottom of the stairs, looking into the kitchen. I could just see both of them—well, Jake and half of Reid.

"Don't get me wrong, mate," Jake said. "I think it's great that you're seeing someone, but you've got to think about something besides yourself this time. People are *missing*."

"Think about something besides *myself this time*?" Reid repeated incredulously. Jake had clearly hit a nerve. "How can you come here and say that to me? You always said I didn't take care of myself or do enough for myself, and now, for the first time, I'm actually taking your advice and then you come here to make me feel guilty for it?"

Jake's expression softened. "I'm sorry, I didn't mean it like that. It's just that if we don't figure this out, there's no saying where or when it'll end. You need to come. Please."

Jake caught sight of me near the stairs then, and Reid turned, following his gaze. He wasn't happy anymore, and his eyes had a hint of defeat in them. He turned back to Jake and nodded. "Fine. I'll be there, just give me a few minutes."

His friend left without another word. I eyed Levi, lying nearby, and was surprised he hadn't reacted at all. He just continued to watch Reid. Maybe our dog really was a dud.

"I take it you have plans?" I asked.

He nodded, not meeting my eyes for long. "I'm sorry. Some things came up and they need my help."

"Does it have to do with the sliders?"

"Yeah . . . at least, we think so." He grabbed his coat from the kitchen chair and pulled it on. "I promise I'll explain everything later, but Jake will come looking for me if I don't meet up with him."

I nodded, trying to hide my disappointment. Reid seemed as though he wanted to say something else, but neither of us spoke, and after a while, he said, "I'll see you later."

He left before I had the chance to say anything, leaving me to stare at the wisps of air and feel the soft breeze blow across my skin. Levi nudged my hand with his nose, and I petted him without thinking.

The rain started up outside and I went upstairs to change back into my sweatpants.

I forced myself to go to bed early, abandoning my movie and dinner, with a dull aching in my stomach that I knew would get worse if I stayed awake. I hoped sleep would take it all away.

I was wrong.

I had nothing to take my mind off my own thoughts and dreams. Images swarmed my mind, and it became hard to concentrate on anything else as the night went on. Long after I climbed into bed, everything became worse. I even started to doubt my own sanity. My mind was a slideshow of images, flipping from one to the other like someone was clicking the button. *Click. Click. Click.*

Paris, Iceland, Mongolia, the middle of the ocean, the top of a building in Tokyo.

Every time the picture changed, the headache became worse. It pounded the back of my skull like the worst migraine imaginable. There came a point when all I could do was shake. I curled up in my bed with my arms wrapped around my legs, wishing for it all to stop. The pain from my stomach seemed to be spreading everywhere, and even my breathing was uneven and labored. I didn't know how much longer I could take it.

Should I go to the hospital? Would they believe me about what I was seeing?

I glanced at the clock; it was only a little after midnight. Thunder continued outside as rain pelted the window. My room was dark and shadowy around me. I couldn't focus on anything specific. The images, the lightning, and trying to distinguish reality was overwhelming.

I grabbed for my phone, thinking maybe I should call Mom or Dad.

A dark shadow passed in front of the window and Reid came into view. Relief coursed through me. I wasn't alone anymore.

He sat down on the edge of my bed and stretched a hand toward my face, but his fingers stopped short, only inches away. "Are you sick again? I thought you were getting better." He pulled his hand away like he wasn't sure if he should touch me, like he was doing something wrong. Maybe worried he would catch whatever I had.

"It always gets worse at night. I don't know why. I think I might have a fever. Is it cold in here?"

He reached his hand toward me again and lightly touched my cheek. "No, you're the one that's cold. Really cold actually."

Reid stood and walked around to the other side of my bed to turn on the nightstand light. He hesitated there, seeing the paper elephant he made sitting next to the lamp. I would have given anything to know his thoughts just then.

When he sat down on the edge of my bed, he brought the scent of grass with him.

"Where did Jake take you?" I asked.

"Upstate New York. I'm sorry I couldn't get back any earlier."

I sat up and leaned against the headboard. With Reid there, it seemed my stomach calmed, and I was able to focus on one thing at a time. Just the smell of the wind he brought put me at ease; it was something easy to focus on.

"When did you start getting sick?" he asked.

"A few days ago, but it wasn't this bad . . . it's getting worse." I didn't think it was the flu any longer.

"It's been getting worse?" I nodded and he thought more. "What does it feel like?"

"It just feels like I'm getting sick. Weaker. But it's not so bad when you're here when I can take my mind off it." Reid was staring at me oddly, like I was telling him something he'd never expected.

"What do you mean by that?" he asked.

I looked down, hesitant to say what was going on with me. It was something not normal. I was afraid to tell him in case he thought I was crazy.

"You can tell me. I promise I'll believe you." There was a short pause. "I need to know, Sam."

At those last words, I looked up, hearing something different in his voice.

I could tell him. I could tell him that my mind had been giving me images that I'd never seen before, places I'd never been to. I could tell him that I thought my dreams and hallucinations were causing my sickness. I was almost sure of it, but how could that be true? And why? Those were the questions that I'd been ignoring for the last week. I was almost scared to know what was wrong with me.

"I think my hallucinations are making me sick," I confessed. Reid stared back at me. "I feel like . . . I feel like I'm losing my mind and everything hurts."

"And when you feel sick, that gets worse when the images happen?"

I nodded. Just thinking about it made my stomach turn again. I could feel it churning deep inside, distraction or not. I knew it was coming again soon. It was to the point where I couldn't stop it. Flashes of different places touched the edges of my vision.

"Do you feel it coming again now?"

"Yes." My voice was weak because I didn't know how much more of it I could take. I just wanted relief and sleep and to have my mind back.

"Sam . . ." He looked at me like he was seeing me for the first time all over again. "I know what's wrong, but . . . Jesus, Sam, haven't your parents told you about this? Don't you realize what's happening?"

The images started coming again. I was on the brink of another wave and I felt like this time I was surely going to drown. My body broke into a cold sweat.

"Told me what?" I asked, now totally confused. My heart raced like I was missing something huge. His words didn't make any sense, and why had he mentioned my parents?

Reid hesitated, gave me a weak smile, and then said, "You're a drifter, Sam."

REID

NEW YORK, UNITED STATES

"YOU'RE A DRIFTER, SAM." AS I SAID THE WORDS, her breath caught in her throat. I was stupid for not seeing the truth sooner. She'd acted so normal, had dismissed her sickness like it was just a small inconvenient thing. She had put on such a brave face that I had believed her.

I should have dug deeper, should have known it was something more. Her body was slowly shutting down, and she hadn't even known it. When I took her drifting, it must have delayed it; it would have relieved the symptoms but not for long.

"How—how do you know?" Her voice was weak with disbelief and her breathing was fast, like she was on the verge of panic. She bent over, hugging her stomach as if she were trying to hold her body together.

I put my hand on her arm, trying to calm her.

"Because we're the same. For the past week, your body has been slowly shutting down because you haven't drifted. Remember what I told you about what happens if I don't drift? What would happen if I continued not to drift?"

She barely nodded. "You'll die."

"And remember what I said about what happens before? You're at that point right now, and if you don't drift, you'll only get worse until you die."

"But that doesn't explain why I'm seeing things."

I was nodding before she ended her sentence. "You're seeing those places because your body is trying to tell you to go there. And the longer you put it off, the worse it'll get. It's like a safety mechanism for your body; it's telling you what it needs. Like someone being thirsty when they need to drink water."

"But the images are of places I've never seen or been to before."

"That's exactly what happens," I told her. "You can think of anywhere in the world, no matter if you've been there or not, and you'll see it as it is, right at that moment."

She suddenly shook her head. "I'm not a drifter, Reid, *you* are! There's no way this is true."

"I promise, it is. I don't know how, but it is. You and I are drifters, Sam."

Sam looked away, trying to understand. I wondered why her parents hadn't told her before now. Her skin was so pale, and she'd probably gotten little to no sleep. Something crossed her face as I looked at her and I knew the pain was coming back.

And it would all go away as soon as she drifted.

My heart raced as I realized that she was just like me. I'd never imagined it would turn out this way.

"Why did you mention my parents?" she asked, uncertain.

"Because it's genetic. Drifting doesn't come randomly. It runs in the family. I don't know who your parents are, but one of them is a drifter."

"Does this mean my brother is, too?"

I opened my mouth, only to pause. "I forgot you had a brother, but yes."

She sighed, dropping her head. "Why do you think they didn't tell me about this? Especially if they *knew* I had it. It doesn't make any sense."

"I don't know."

Sam took a shaky breath. It wasn't hard to guess what was going through her mind. In a matter of moments, she had been plunged into a world she knew nothing of other than the glimpses I had given her. It was a lot to take in.

She needed to drift. My first time drifting has never left my memory. It was the most terrifying and exhilarating moment of my life. Even if it had been an accident.

"Sam."

When she looked at me, her eyes were darker than before, like the pain within was spreading everywhere.

I'd never experienced what she was going through, but I'd heard stories. Every drifter has.

"So I really have to do this?" she asked quietly.

I tried to give her a smile, nodding. "You're making it sound like it's a bad thing."

Sam was almost to the point of shaking again, and her fingers gripped her blanket like it was the only thing she had to hold on to. "I don't know if I can do it, Reid."

A tear ran down her cheek. I didn't even think as I moved closer to her, to the point where I was sitting right beside her, facing her with only inches between us. I put my hands over hers. They were cold. I felt a nervous rush run through my veins being close to her, but I made myself look into her eyes and nowhere else. They held a fear of the unknown. I felt the urge to look away, but I fought it and never broke eye contact.

"Drifting is nothing to be afraid of," I told her. "It should be the opposite. You know the feeling when I took you along with me for the first time? It's so much better than that. It can't even compare when you do it yourself." She still didn't seem convinced. I didn't know what else to say. So I told her the only thing that came to my mind. "It's who you are. When you drift, you'll realize that. It'll be like completing one of your puzzles: you'll see the whole picture for the first time and it will all make sense."

Something in her eyes brightened, which was what I'd been hoping for. She needed to see this wasn't a bad thing—it was a gift. She also needed to experience it for herself to fall in love with it. After that, she would never doubt again.

I realized my hands were still over hers, and I pulled them away.

"Why didn't I feel better when I went drifting with you that night?" she asked. "Shouldn't that have taken it away?"

"No, it needs to be you. When you go with me, I'm the one drifting, and you're just along for the ride. To make this all go away, you have to perform the action yourself."

She seemed surer this time and gave me a small nod. I could tell she was nervous, but that was the predrift jitters. That's what Dad had always called it. Before my heart could sink at the thought of him, I said, "Come on, you should do it before you get any worse."

Neither of us moved and I waited.

"Where will I go?" she asked.

"Wherever you want, but I do have a question. What's the one place that keeps coming to your mind over everything else?"

Sam didn't hesitate, already knowing the answer. "Cliffs, somewhere near the ocean."

"Where?" The corner of my mouth lifted when she looked up at me.

"What do you mean, where?"

"Think about it again and tell me where." I knew she could find out, she just had to simply think about it.

"It's in Ireland."

I nodded, smiling. "That's your drift point, then. Everyone has one. It's the place you go when you have no time to think of somewhere else. It's like your personal homing beacon. If you drift without thinking, you'll go there. Some of them make sense, like somewhere from your past, but others are just random. Jake's drift point is an alleyway in Cuba. It's the weirdest thing. The neighboring kitchen knows him quite well."

Sam smiled at that and asked, "Where's your drift point?"

My smile faltered a bit, but I shrugged, hoping she wouldn't notice. "A field in Finland, of all places. Nothing worth talking about." I stood up from the bed and looked down at her. "Are you ready?"

She hesitated for a moment before saying, "Yeah, I think I am."

SAM

NEW YORK, UNITED STATES

IT HAD TO BE SOME SORT OF JOKE. THERE WAS no way we—I, my family—were drifters and I had never known about it.

But if Reid was right, if all of this was what he said it was? Why hadn't they told me? Why?

I pushed those thoughts from my mind and focused on the here and now.

I stood next to Reid with my stomach turning, not knowing what to do. I had gotten dressed in something more appropriate than shorts and a T-shirt, and I definitely stalled in the process. Nerves clawed at my stomach and I felt like I might throw up. If it was true, then this wasn't just an upset stomach, and my body was shutting down. I was *dying*.

But not for long. I was about to do something I hadn't known anyone to be capable of until two days earlier.

"How do I do it?" I asked again.

"You just do." There was a hint of a smile in his voice. "Think about the place and then let yourself go. It'll be like coming up for air after being underwater."

"You make it sound easy."

"It *is* easy." There was a laugh in his voice, making it raspier than usual.

I looked at him one more time, trying to gain enough courage. I felt ridiculous standing in my room, thinking I was about to appear in an entirely different country. The pain in my stomach came again and my head felt like it was splitting apart.

I just wanted it to *stop*.

"You'll be right behind me?"

"Yes, but you have to take the leap yourself."

He was right. This *was* something I had to do myself. I thought about closing my eyes, but I found that I *wanted* to see this. I barely had to think of the place; it came effortlessly.

The image of the cliffs and ocean came so clearly. The black sky was just beginning to become light with dawn. My heart pounded so hard I thought it would explode. When I saw the place as clearly as I saw my bedroom, I stepped forward.

And nothing happened.

I turned back to Reid, whose eyebrow was raised. "Huh."

"What do you mean, *huh*?" My voice was one pitch higher than it should have been. "That's all you have to say?"

He shook his head, almost laughing. I didn't think anything was funny about it. "You're thinking too much," he said

"What—"

He pushed me forward, cutting off my words. They were still lingering in my mouth when the image of him faded. My stomach dropped like I was free-falling, like I was going down a roller coaster at a dangerous speed, everything all at once. The air caught in my throat for the moment I was in between places.

When I could breathe again, I stood where I'd always imagined, where I'd been dreaming of. The water far below me, crashing against the rocks, and the sky still dark with hints of red on the horizon. The wind blew through my hair and clothes and that's when the realization hit me:

I did it. I drifted.

Reid was right. The pain in my stomach was gone, replaced with a sense of feeling whole, even though I had never known anything had been missing. I felt *alive*. I felt like I could fly.

I looked out across the ocean and realized something else—this was only the beginning. Without a plane, boat, or train, I could go wherever I wanted. I could finally travel, like I'd always wanted to, in a way that I had never known existed. The world was at my fingertips and all I had to do was take a single step.

"You did it."

"You pushed me," I said without looking over my shoulder

"Uh, yeah, sorry about that." Even though he apologized, he still smiled.

"I guess it worked, didn't it?"

"It looks that way."

"Do you think you'll have trouble doing it again?" he asked.

I shook my head, already knowing the answer. "No, but do you always have to step forward to do it?"

"No, I just wanted to give you the basic idea so you wouldn't overthink it." He smiled at that, knowing I had anyway. "But you can drift as long as you're moving, even if the motion is really small. When you move your arm, it still disrupts the air, and that's about the amount of movement you need. Or you could do the opposite and jump off a building. All you need to do is find a breeze to ride on."

Find a breeze to ride on. He had an odd way of explaining it, but I understood all the same. "You've jumped off a building?"

"Cliff, building, it's all the same. But it's twice the rush."

"I don't think I'm ready to jump off a building yet."

"No, don't. You'll get the knack of drifting in no time. It's a part of you, but take your time trying new stuff until you're ready."

"Like fighting?"

"Like fighting," Reid agreed with a small smile, causing the tiniest hint of his dimple to appear.

I watched him out of the corner of my eye for a moment. His hair blew across his forehead in the breeze. He was the only reason I knew anything about this world and where I fit into it. And thinking about it made me realize how little I knew of it.

"Will you tell me more about the sliders?" I asked. "What are you guys so worried about?"

"Things have gotten complicated between us," he started. "We've always been at odds with each other, but it's getting worse."

"They can slow time?"

"Yeah, so if you see them coming, they just look like a blur. Too fast for you to see or react. So if you don't drift fast enough, it'll be too late. Once they're close to you, you won't stand a chance."

"Like that night of the fight? When that guy had the knife to your ribs, you couldn't go anywhere because he would be faster than you?"

"As soon as he felt me move or try to drift, he would have killed me." He looked over. "Make sure you never take chances like that. Don't ever think you're fast enough to escape them when they're close to you."

I nodded, not having any words. "So they've been giving everyone trouble?"

"Drifters have been disappearing, and we think a man named Knox is behind it. You could say he's the unofficial leader of the sliders."

That made me pause. "Drifters are disappearing?"

"Yes, and for some reason, we can't find them," Reid said.

"What do you mean by that?"

"It's the ability that comes with drifting," he explained. "Instead of thinking of a place to drift to, you can think of the person. A friend or family, but sometimes you can even find someone you've never met if you know their name and what they look like."

All I could think was *wow*. "So if you wanted to, you could find the president and just . . . *drift* to him?"

Reid nodded. "I mean, that would probably be a death sentence with all his security, but yes, you could. But it only comes with practice."

"So with all these people disappearing . . . nobody can find them?"

"Yeah, it seems to be the case. We're just . . . we're hoping they're not dead."

I looked at him sharply. "Sliders could be killing them?" I whispered.

"We don't think so, but the possibility is there."

"Not the greatest time to be a new drifter, huh?" I joked half-heartedly. What sort of world had I just become a part of?

"I'm sure it'll blow over. It always does." Reid took a deep breath and looked over. "We should go back. You should get some sleep after the night you've had."

"Yeah, probably," I agreed.

But Reid paused, looking at me a moment long enough for me to wonder if he wanted to kiss me. The thought sent sparks down into my stomach.

Then he looked away and asked, "I'll meet you outside on the steps, all right?"

I nodded, wishing he would meet me inside instead. But he was right; I did need sleep, and if he came inside, I wouldn't want him to leave.

This time I had no trouble drifting.

Like Reid had promised, it was like breathing.

SAM

NEW YORK, UNITED STATES

REID WAS THERE WAITING FOR ME ON THE BOT-tom step when I appeared with my small rush of wind. It was really early in the morning, the sky still black, which made me remember I had school the next day. I grimaced at the thought.

"What's with the face?" Reid asked.

"I have school today."

He snorted. "Good luck with that. At least you'll get a few hours of sleep before then."

I nodded, admitting, "It'll be nice to sleep again. Maybe my dreams will be normal for once." My cell phone buzzed in my pocket and I sighed, pulling it out, expecting to see something from Nella that perhaps hadn't delivered when I was outside my service range. "It's a voice mail from my mom." I debated whether to listen to it right then. I didn't want to, afraid that Reid would leave too soon, but I hadn't heard from my mom since the day before yesterday.

"Are you going to listen to it?"

"I will when I go inside." I shoved my phone back in my

pocket and looked back up at Reid. He was hesitating, not knowing what to do or say.

"See you later?" I asked.

"Yeah, of course." He grinned.

I slowly turned away, still reluctant. I thought maybe he would stop me—*hoped* he would stop me. He didn't. When I was at the top step, he said, "Sam?"

"Yeah?" I glanced over my shoulder, just to see him breathing a bit heavy.

"I—I've been having a really great time with you, and—" He was lost for words, unable to say anything.

I nodded in return, knowing exactly what he meant. "Me too."

A hint of another smile appeared and he nodded once.

I unlocked the door and went inside, not turning back to see him disappear. It had become something I didn't like seeing, no matter the brilliance of it. Levi licked my hand the moment the door shut, and I let out a long breath. It was the oddest thing, being back inside the same house but not being the same person.

I was about to go upstairs but I paused, thinking about my options. I could walk up the steps, the same as usual, or I could be extremely lazy.

I smiled, thinking of the latter.

My alarm clock went off for a good ten minutes before I was able to quiet it. I sat up in bed and rubbed at my heavy eyes. I looked down and groaned. I hadn't even undressed before going to bed. My legs were tangled with my comforter from the result of having jeans on the whole night. My entire body felt dirty and too warm.

I let out an audible groan.

At least I wasn't sick anymore—it was so much a relief that I actually smiled, right there and then. I'd never felt more like myself.

I checked my phone and realized I had never checked the voice mail from Mom last night. It was probably nothing important anyway, but it wasn't like me to forget. I quickly listened.

"Sam, it's me." Her voice sounded shaky and out of breath, like she was going up a flight of stairs. *"I need you to call me as soon as you get this, all right? Not a moment later."* There was a pause. *"I love you, Sam."*

My eyebrows creased as I pulled the phone away. Mom never left me messages like that, *ever*. Thinking about her made me realize again that she had never told me about drifting. Why hadn't she *told* me? Why hadn't either of them? Just like Reid had said, they must have had their reasons.

At least, that's what I wanted to believe.

I tried to call Mom back. It rang about seven times before the voice mail came on. I left a quick message saying to call me back, but even after I hung up, I had a bad feeling about it. I couldn't ever remember not being able to reach Mom.

The voice mail she left me put a bad taste in my mouth.

I was showered and redressed fifteen minutes later. And again, instead of walking downstairs, I drifted straight into the kitchen. My hair ruffled when I appeared and Levi just stared at me from the hallway, waiting for his breakfast.

No wonder he doesn't think it's strange.

When Reid and Jake were here, the dog didn't respond any differently to their odd ways of coming and going. Right then I knew why—he was already used to either Mom or Dad, and maybe even Logan, doing the same thing. It was normal to him.

The thought made me more bitter than before.

Why didn't they tell me?

I walked to the subway as I normally would have, making it to school just on time. The day was a blur and my lack of sleep the last few nights hadn't helped. School was the last thing I wanted to focus on.

Reid wouldn't stay out of my head for more than a few minutes at a time, and I couldn't help but wonder when he would show up again. I half expected him on the subway this morning, but he never showed.

When school was over a little after three o'clock, I walked drearily to the coffee shop to meet Nella. The weather matched my mood and rain threatened to come down at any minute. I regretted telling her I would meet up. I just wanted to go home. But it was inevitable that we were going to talk about the boy she'd discovered in my house.

I pulled out my phone and tried to call Mom again and it went straight to voice mail. I was starting to get worried.

I tried calling Dad next, for good measure, and I went to his voice mail, too.

The bell over the door dinged as I walked inside the shop. Nella was already waiting at our table with her arms crossed, eyes on fire. I sat down gingerly. Finally, after a few minutes of silence, I couldn't take it anymore.

"I'm sorry, all right?" I blurted out. "But it's not like you told me about Luke either."

"So you decided to give me a taste of my own medicine?" Her eyes narrowed behind her glasses. "Nice, Sam, I really appreciate it."

"It's not like I've known him for a while. Only since last week."

Her eyebrows pulled together. "*Last week?* Moving a little fast, don't you think?"

The fact that that was the first thing she thought of—us moving too fast—was hurtful. She didn't bother asking where we met, or what he was like. She didn't care about him. She just cared that I hadn't told her right away.

"It's not like we *did* anything. He came over because I wasn't feeling well."

"I thought I was the one you called if you were sick or had cramps."

"Nell—" I closed my mouth, hating this conversation more and more. Sure, maybe I should have thrown her a text, but my life had been a little more than hectic lately. "I thought you would understand. I'm sure you don't want me there, hanging over your and Luke's relationship every step of the way. Am I right?"

"You still could have told me sooner," she said again, giving me a bit more attitude than she normally would have. "I don't like coming to your house and finding out that you've replaced me with a boy you don't even know."

Before I had time to respond, she got up and walked out the door. I was left speechless and on the verge of crying out of anger. We'd had our arguments, but it had never gotten to the point where one of us had walked away before. I didn't want to chase after her and tell her I was sorry. I'd already done that—she hadn't accepted it.

I sat at the table a moment longer before leaving, stepping out into the overcast weather again. I felt lost. I couldn't get a hold of my parents, and now Nella wouldn't talk to me. I hadn't seen Reid yet either, and that was bothering me more than anything. I just wanted to go somewhere, anywhere but here or home . . . and I *could*.

But where?

People walked past me on the street, a few cussing because I was in their way, bumping into my still form because I wouldn't move. I thought about Logan. I hadn't seen him since August, and that was all the reason I needed to persuade myself to pay him a visit. Maybe I would get lucky and he could tell me why Mom and Dad never told me about us—about *me*.

I'd been to his campus once, and that memory was enough for me to get a clear picture of where I wanted to go. I picked a spot near the outside of his building, on the corner where nobody would see me appear. Reid had yet to explain how nobody ever saw him drift. He obviously did it in public, and yet nobody ever seemed to notice him.

I made a mental note to ask the next time I saw him.

A nervous jitter ran through me before taking that initial step. My stomach turned over as my surroundings changed. The thrill was still new, and I thought it was impossible I'd ever get used to it.

When I appeared, it was drizzling and the grass was wet. People scurried from the buildings with umbrellas over their heads. I pulled up my hood and started off across the lawn toward the dorm's entrance. The halls were noisy when I stepped inside. It was full of guys, and the smell of sweat and unwashed laundry hung heavily in the air. Music echoed off the walls from somewhere.

A few guys glanced at me as I made my way through the crowded hall, but I was able to make it to Logan's door unscathed. I knocked a few times and waited. A guy leaned up against the wall, talking to a friend of his, but he looked over, trying to appear casual. His eyes roamed.

I looked away and knocked again. The door opened a moment later, but it wasn't Logan who stood before me. The guy was in the middle of brushing his teeth and pulling on a jacket. His light hair was messy and still wet from a shower. He raised his eyebrows when he saw me.

"Who are you?" He narrowed his eyes. "If Jeff sent you, tell him I was totally kidding last night."

I grimaced. "Um, no. I'm Logan's sister."

126

He stopped brushing his teeth and pointed at me with his toothbrush. "You're Sam?"

I nodded. "Is Logan here?"

"No, he went somewhere last night, and I don't think he's been back. Here, come on in."

He opened the door wider, and I stepped inside. I couldn't help but notice that Logan's side of the room was a little neater than his roommate's. Our mom rubbed off on us, apparently.

"Do you have any idea when he'll be back?" I asked.

He spit his toothpaste into the trash can and finished putting on his jacket. "I have no idea, but I wouldn't try calling him. He left his phone." He gestured over to the nightstand next to Logan's bed. "I've gotta to go, but feel free to hang out and wait for him if you want. Just shut the door on your way out."

I muttered a thanks as he left. I went over to his bed and sat down, grabbing Logan's phone from the table. *Why would he leave his phone?* I swiped it open, put in the same password our whole family used, and looked at the recent text messages, thinking that would give me hints that would help me find him. After finding nothing, I looked at his calls. Mom had called him last night, around the same time she'd called me.

Again, *what the heck?* It was like they all decided to go on vacation but forgot to invite me along.

"Wanna party tonight?" The guy from the hallway stood leaning against the door, wearing a smile that I presumed was supposed to win me over.

"No."

"Just *no*?" He unfolded his arms and took a step inside the room. "You won't even give me a chance? Come on." He smiled. "You'll have a good time."

What kind of school had parties on the weekdays? I placed Logan's phone on his stand and stood. The guy flashed another smile, thinking I was about to agree to go somewhere with him.

"No, thanks."

I walked past him and didn't bother staying around to shut the door.

Since nobody was in the next hallway, I used that chance to leave. I wanted to go somewhere else besides home—where I was constantly reminded that I knew nothing about anything—so I quickly thought of a location in London. I'd always wanted to go to England, so why not now?

It had to be around eleven o'clock in London when I drifted into the dark alleyway, and the rain was coming down hard. A moment after I arrived, I leaned against one of the walls, breathing deeply, not getting enough air. My hands shook as I lowered myself to the ground and let myself cry. Luckily, there was an overhang and I had found the only dry place to sit down.

I had no idea where my parents were, or Logan for that matter, and Nella wouldn't even talk to me. I felt lost, even though I knew exactly where I was every minute of the day.

Cars drove past the mouth of the alleyway, and a few people dotted the sidewalks. Nobody noticed me. I knew I was being stupid and wasting time with my tears. But I had never been through so much over the span of a few days before, and I felt overwhelmed and scared. Logan was the one person I could always count on to be there for me. Someone I could talk to when I didn't feel like talking to my parents.

And he wasn't there.

I closed my eyes and thought of him really hard, thinking I could find him the same way I drifted. But I only saw black. The same happened when I thought of Mom and Dad, but didn't Reid say it came with practice?

A sound rang out down the alley—a familiar breeze that made me feel a little less alone. Reid crouched next to me, and I finally lifted my head, my eyes going straight for him like there was nothing else I wanted to look at. His eyes were dark with the night, concern written all over him.

"I haven't had the best day," I told him.

"That's obvious." He shifted his weight and sat down next to me under the overhang, getting out of the rain. I felt calmer with him there—less alone. The day's events caught up with me again now that I was sitting there, nothing else to think on.

"I went to visit Logan."

"Your brother?"

"Yeah, but he wasn't there. His roommate said he left sometime last night and never came back. He left his phone— he *never* leaves his phone. But that's not the weird thing. The weird thing is that he talked to my mom last night, around the same time she left me a voice mail."

"You still haven't gotten hold of her, then?"

"No." A lump lodged in my throat as I worried about what might be happening. "I can't find them," I voiced. "I've even tried finding them by drifting, but it didn't work."

"That only comes with practice, trust me. You'll get there."

"And in the meantime?"

"Well, I might be able to do it. Do you have pictures of them?"

I pulled out my phone and found a few pictures of my parents. Reid scrolled through them and then he closed his eyes for a moment, his eyebrows furrowing. He glanced at me and then tried again, finally shaking his head.

Then he said, almost like he didn't want to, "Something is wrong . . . I can't find them either."

I remembered what Reid said.

"Reid, you said drifters were going missing. What if—"

I couldn't even finish the sentence. Could it be coincidence?

Reid saw the look on my face and said in a hurry, "Hey, just because I can't see them doesn't mean we can't find them. It'll be okay."

I could only nod and asked, "Has that ever happened before?"

He didn't answer and just said, "I promise we'll figure this out."

Reid reached his hand over and twined his fingers with mine. He was a lot warmer than I was, and without even thinking about it, I leaned my head on his shoulder. It was probably the closest we'd ever been. I wanted more.

"You'll get used to this world," he told me. "It's different for you because you started later than usual. It's a lot to take in. But you already fit in perfectly. You'll see."

I remained silent, not wanting to ruin his flawless words but still worrying about my family. The weather caught up to me, and I shivered in response to the cold.

"You should probably go home before you get sick. How long have you been here?"

"Not long."

He got up and offered his hand to help me up. He didn't let go and I squeezed tighter.

We drifted back to the front of my house. The streets were damp with rain from earlier that day, and evening was coming on fast. My hand was still in Reid's, but this time he didn't pull away.

"I'll go find Jake, see if he knows anything about your parents or brother. Just please try not to worry too much." He showed me a smile that made my heart pound. "And get some sleep. You look like you need it."

"Thanks," I said, my sarcastic tone coming out. "Every girl loves hearing that, especially from a guy."

"Would it make a difference if I said that you still looked great?"

"Not unless it's true."

He nodded. "It's true." His eyes trailed down to our hands, as if he'd forgotten he was still holding mine.

Reid hesitated for a moment before stepping forward and placing a soft kiss on my cheek, almost at the corner of my mouth. I didn't have the courage to turn into him. He lingered there for a moment, his mouth next to my ear, and a warm shiver ran down my spine. "You have no idea how badly I want to kiss you," he murmured. "Maybe next time, okay?"

I nodded. "Next time."

He smirked as he stepped back, drifting when he did, and he was gone.

A stupid smile was plastered on my face. I gave my heart a few moments to calm down before going into the house. It was quiet inside, as usual, and the only lights I had left on were right over the entryway and above the stove. It glowed dimly from the kitchen as usual, but then something caught my eye.

The back door had been shattered and bits of glass covered the floor. I froze instantly, not knowing what to do. I tried to take calming breaths, and after a short while, I was able to move forward, slowly.

Levi was nowhere in sight, which worried me. He was always here, always ready to greet me at the door. The house was silent, and I stopped midway down the dark hall. Someone had broken in, that was all. They were probably long gone, and Levi was outside still trying to pick up their scent.

It was hard to convince myself of that. I was too scared to move farther into the house, or even make another sound. My heart pounded too hard and my breathing too fast. Would it be horrible if I drifted away and got help? Reid would know what to do.

My phone. I needed to call the police.

That thought was the last thing my brain registered before my world became chaos.

Light flashed around me like lightning, blinding me and making my ears ring. I blinked and blinked but saw nothing

131

but white. I dropped to the floor, a mute scream coming from my throat. Something cold snapped around my wrist and I jerked back, still unable to hear or see.

I tried to drift.

I couldn't.

SAM

NEW YORK, UNITED STATES

MY VISION WAS WHITE FOR A LONG TIME, AND then, slowly, I started to see bits of color. Blurry figures stood over me, and I could barely breathe. Everything was still muted—I could hear nothing but the loud ringing in my ears. Someone turned on all the lights and the hallway finally lit up, coming into focus. The first thing I saw was my phone, smashed on the floor next to me.

Then I saw a man standing above me. He talked and gestured toward me with his hands, but every word he spoke sounded muffled and unclear. After the initial shock wore off, I thought about moving—at least off my back where I felt too vulnerable.

In one smooth motion, I flipped over and pushed myself against the wall. My back had barely touched it when something yanked on my wrist, jerking me to a stop. A metal cuff was clasped around it, connected to a chain. A chain that was bolted straight into the hardwood floor.

Was this why I couldn't drift? When I tried, I saw the place I wanted to go, but I couldn't go there. It was like the chain was anchoring me here. Reid hadn't told me there were rules to drifting as well as limitations. Was this one of them?

The man crouched down in front of me. I recognized him from the night of the fight. Reid said his name—was it Butch? Bill? Something with a B. After a minute, my ears stopped ringing. Voices came from the living room and the kitchen. Everywhere in the house. There were more of them here than I could see.

The man leaned in and sniffed my hair. "Hmm, drifter. Just as I thought." He tilted his head and I didn't respond, not that it mattered to him. "This is all new to you, isn't it? Nobody ever told you that you can't drift when you're connected to something you can't take with you, huh?"

He stood up and yelled toward the kitchen. "Gavin! Come unbolt her so we can be on our way."

He left for the living room and more voices greeted him, one speaking his name, *Buck*. That's what it was. Who were these people and why were they here?

A guy around my age emerged from the kitchen, not looking happy about being there. His face looked set in stone with his lips pressed into a thin line. He grabbed my wrist a little too hard and turned it over. The cuff clicked open and dropped to the floor.

Gavin, I presumed, pulled me to my feet and his hand clung to my arm.

"Don't try to drift," he warned. "I'll be right here if you do."

He led me into the living room and his grip stayed tight, like he expected me to try drifting at any moment. Maybe I should. What would he do if I did? Maybe I could drift and get away from him in time to drift again, leaving him wherever I wanted.

There were four more people in the living room, two men and two women, staring at me. He brought me to the far side where Buck was. Why were so many of them here?

Buck leveled his gaze on me and asked, "Do you have any idea where your parents are?"

That made me pause—why was he asking about my parents? I swallowed away my dry mouth and said, "I don't know. Who are you? What are you doing in our house? What do you *want*?"

He ignored my questions. Buck turned to the others and said, "Let's go."

Something suddenly appeared in my peripheral vision, bringing along with it the sound I've come to know so well. When I turned to look, everything and everybody exploded into action.

Gavin pushed me from behind and I fell to the ground, my face hitting the floor hard, white flashing behind my eyes. I couldn't see what was going on—nothing but wood and dust from under the couch. His knee pressed into my back and I gritted my teeth. Buck and another man yelled, and the sound of scrambling feet was everywhere.

"Hold him down!" There was more shuffling and the sound of a punch. "Gavin, throw me those cuffs."

He did and then, almost too quiet for me to hear, Gavin cursed under his breath.

My heart hammered into the floor, and his knee was still pressed against my back, but I wiggled underneath him and was able to move my head so I could see what was happening.

It was Reid.

REID

TOKYO, JAPAN

AFTER I HAD LEFT SAM ON HER DOORSTEP, I'D gone to find Jake. I needed to find more info about Sam's parents. Jake was on the corner of a busy street in Tokyo, waiting with other people to cross. It was hard to drift into a crowd that big without freaking someone out, but all I got was a glare from someone when I accidentally bumped their shoulder.

Cell phones were amazing distractions.

Jake glanced over at me, not saying anything. Everyone started across the street, and once we were out of the big crowd, Jake finally started talking.

"You've got to start being more careful," he said. "I know you won't leave the city, but I wish you would. There's too many sliders in New York."

"I'm careful enough." We walked down the sidewalk, but my mind was somewhere else. "I have to ask you something."

"What is it?"

"I was wondering if you knew anything about Sam's parents."

He stopped and turned to me. "Why would I know something about her parents?"

"Sam found out last night that she's a drifter, but they never told her anything. Now they're missing. They've been gone for a few days and now she can't get ahold of them. I'm worried they've gone missing with the others."

Jake stared blankly at something across the street, and I could sense that his mind was reeling.

"What are their names?" he finally asked.

"Alex and Chloe?"

Jake cursed and he nodded. "Yeah, they're missing, along with their son. Within the last day."

"And nobody still has any idea where they are? Why can't we find them?"

Jake turned on me suddenly, his voice more angry than usual. "That's what I've been trying to tell you, Reid. Do you not listen to anything I say?"

"I'm sorry," I told him. "I'm sorry I haven't been . . . here. I should have been."

He deflated some, shaking his head. "It wouldn't have mattered. We can't find the missing drifters because something is blocking us from seeing them or . . . or they're dead."

I thought about trying to find Sam's parents—only seeing black. "Do we know which it is?"

Jake shrugged. "We aren't sure. Things are . . . things aren't looking promising right now."

I'd never seen Jake look so defeated before. This was way more serious than I had first thought.

I finally asked the question: "So what is everyone doing about it?"

Jake was silent for too long, only to answer with, "We're hiding."

So that's why he was in Tokyo? *Hiding*?

"So you're just giving up?"

He whirled on me again. "Don't pretend to care, Reid,

because you never did before now. Sure, you came with me *once* and the whole time you weren't even listening."

If he had punched me in the gut, it probably would have felt better. I'd been so busy with Sam that I kept brushing off Jake. I was a shitty friend.

"I'm sorry."

He turned away and I grabbed his shoulder. "Jake, wait."

"I'm going home," he said. "I'm tired. Go tell your girlfriend about her parents and hope they don't come for her next."

That hadn't even occurred to me. My mind automatically went to Sam, and the image that came made me flinch back. All the air left my lungs. "They're already there," I whispered, my heart kicking up a notch.

Jake stared at me, silently screaming at me not to do something stupid because he knew me too well. I was great at doing stupid things.

"I have to go," I said.

"Reid, you *can't*. You'll be bolted before you can ever get to her."

I shook my head. "I don't care. I'm going." I couldn't lie, I was nervous. I couldn't break the tension in my stomach no matter how hard I tried. I was about to give myself over to the sliders but not without a fight. I couldn't sit by and do nothing.

"Don't do this." He grabbed my shoulders. "Don't hand yourself to them. They've got too many of us already."

I swallowed hard. "She would do the same for me."

"You know I can't come for you," Jake said. "I won't be able to find you."

"I know." I gave him a nod. "It's okay."

The hardness in his eyes left, but he also didn't have words for me. There *were* no words. I wasn't even sure if I would see him again.

I acted before thinking, because I knew what I had to do.

SAM

NEW YORK, UNITED STATES

WHAT WAS HE THINKING, COMING HERE? HE HAD to know he would be caught, but he showed up anyway.

Two men held him to the floor, using their weight to keep him in place. My stomach turned, wishing he hadn't come. I struggled against Gavin, wanting to help Reid, but all he did was put more weight against me.

After a moment, when Reid was finally restrained, with barely room to breathe, Buck barked out a laugh.

"Reid, fancy seeing you here," he said. "What did Jake say last time? That you'd be on your own the next time I saw you?"

Reid struggled against the men holding him down, and Buck motioned for them to let him let up. They grabbed his shoulders and pulled him to his feet. Gavin did the same for me, not letting go of my arm as I pushed myself up.

Reid breathed heavily and he glanced at me, pain and regret filling his eyes.

He looked at Buck and asked, "What are you doing here?" his voice rougher than usual.

"I could ask you the same thing," said Buck. "You lied to

me the other night, Reid. You told me she was *nobody*—that she didn't know anything."

"She *didn't*."

Buck made a face like he didn't believe him. Then he turned to the others. "Let's go."

The others took Reid out the front door and Gavin pulled me along behind them. For once, I wished our street wasn't so quiet. There was nobody here to witness us being taken.

Two black SUVs idled at the curb, and Reid and I exchanged a glance before they put us into separate vehicles.

Throughout the whole trip, Gavin's hand stayed around my arm and he never said a word. I was just glad Buck wasn't in this car—but then regretted thinking it, because it meant he was with Reid.

They didn't bother with a blindfold, or prevent me seeing where we were going, so it was obvious we were headed toward Huntington on Long Island. We passed huge mansions and other properties hidden by gates and hedges. Expensive properties that couldn't be seen from the road.

Not much later, we were following a long road to a big house surrounded by trees. They pulled into the circular driveway in front of a huge porch and got us out. Reid had two men on either side of him, but he was staring at the house like he'd seen it before.

They brought us inside where only a few lights were on, illuminating the large paintings on the walls and the huge staircase wrapping along the right wall. They kept us moving, down a wide hallway, past multiple doors, and into a huge office with full bookshelves and a flat-screen TV hanging in the corner.

I glanced behind me quickly, catching Reid's eye. He didn't try to smile or nod, and I realized it was because he was nervous. It wasn't reassuring.

There was a man sitting on one of the couches by the fireplace, reading something on his iPad.

Buck said, "Knox."

The man looked up and I finally made the connection. *This* was Knox? The man who was supposedly taking drifters? The leader of the sliders? No wonder Reid was nervous—we were in his *house.*

His short hair had tinges of gray in it, but he appeared to be no older than my dad. He was tall, too, even taller than Buck, who stood a head taller than Reid and had a sharp look about him, an aura that spoke of confidence and intelligence.

"Any trouble?" Knox asked, his eyes gazing over us. They lingered over Reid a little while longer, curiosity striking.

"No trouble," Buck told him. "Gavin was quick."

Knox finally stood and came over to take a closer look.

"And I see you've brought an extra guest?"

"This one came to us."

Knox raised an eyebrow and looked at Reid. "What's your name?"

When Reid didn't say anything right away, Buck slapped the back of his head and, surprisingly, Knox got angry about it. He grabbed Buck's shoulder and said, so low I could barely hear, "Wait outside."

Buck hesitated, looking like he wanted to say something, then left Reid's side and walked out the door.

Knox looked at everyone else and said, "Give us the room, and free his hands."

Gavin finally let go of my arm and unlocked the cuffs around Reid's wrists. Knox gestured toward the couch and took a seat at the opposite one. Everyone else left the room except Gavin, taking a standing position behind Knox.

I glanced at Reid, wondering if we could drift before they stopped us. He caught my eye like he was thinking the same.

"Please," Knox said, seeing our hesitation. "If you leave now, you'll never find your parents."

I took a sharp breath and turned to him. "What did you say?"

"Your parents are missing, right?"

"Yeah, because of *you*." I was surprised at the anger in my voice but asked anyway, "Where are they?"

Knox had the audacity to look confused.

I took a step closer, ready to do something I'd regret, and Reid stopped me with a hand around my wrist.

"Sam, wait." Reid glanced at Knox and said, "Maybe we should hear him out."

"*Hear him out*? He took my parents and brother."

Reid finally looked away from Knox and whispered in my ear, "I don't think he did."

I looked back at the man on the couch, wondering if anything he told me would be the truth. I couldn't trust anything he said, could I?

"How do we know you didn't take them?" I asked.

Knox sighed and answered, "Because long ago, your father and I used to be friends."

Knox and my dad were . . . friends? "Why would my dad be friends with *you*? My dad would never hang out with someone who kidnaps teenagers or hires other people to do his dirty work."

Knox tilted his head back, studying me. "They didn't tell you anything, did they?" He gestured to the couch again. "Please, sit, and I will try my best to explain."

We sat and I was glad Reid was close to me, giving me more courage than I would have had alone. He kept glancing at Gavin, and I wondered who he thought was the bigger threat in the room.

"What have your parents told you?" Knox asked, bringing back my attention.

"Nothing."

His eyebrows knitted together. "Nothing? Not even of their past or—"

Reid interrupted. "She didn't know anything until I told her she was a drifter barely even a day ago. Her parents left for the weekend and she got sick, and that's when I figured it out."

"What's your name?"

"Reid."

Knox asked me again, "So they told you absolutely nothing?"

"Yes."

Knox just said, "Hmm."

I let out a breath. "That's all you have to say?"

Knox shrugged. "He always said he would try, but I never knew if he ever went through with it."

"Try *what*?"

"Not telling you, for your own safety." Knox leaned forward, elbows on knees. "As you can imagine, in our world, the longer someone doesn't know they're a drifter, the less danger they're in. By not telling you, your parents delayed the process of your ability manifesting."

Then Reid said the same thing. "Hmm." I gave him a look and he actually *smiled*. "Sorry, it's just . . . I never thought of it that way. I'm sure they always planned to be there for you when you got sick, but under the circumstances, they couldn't."

"Because they were *taken*." I turned back to Knox. "How do I know you didn't take them? Everyone knows you hate drifters."

Knox spread out his palms and said, "Everyone knows we have our differences, yes, but your father wasn't a drifter. And even though he married one and we lost touch, I still care about him."

I opened my mouth, but no words came out, because *what*? It was like my mind was suddenly a sticky cloud and nothing made any sense. Thankfully, Reid made the connection for me.

He said, "He's a slider? But—only drifters have been disappearing."

Knox nodded once. "That's true . . . until your father, Sam. Probably because he and your mother were together, but I can't say for sure. But the fact is—we didn't take them and we don't know who did."

"Then why are we here?" Reid asked, voicing my own thoughts.

For a moment, I felt lightheaded and just focused on breathing, then focused on listening to what Knox had to say and tried not to think about anything else. Knox was sure the missing drifters were still alive, but what if he was wrong?

"I sent for Sam because I think she might be able to help." Knox looked at me and, again, even that was too much to take in. "Her family is missing and I couldn't think of any other drifter who would be willing to talk with me."

"You could have asked," I said. "You know, instead of kid-napping me?"

"Would you have said yes?" Then Knox smiled because he saw the look on my face. "I didn't think so. I'm sorry we had to be so . . . abrupt."

Reid interjected, sounding angrier than before. "So you only care about the missing drifters because your friend is missing with them? How noble."

"I never said I was a good man, Reid. But with this whole situation, I feel responsible."

I narrowed my eyes. "How so?"

Knox stood and walked over to the corner of the room. It was like a scene from a movie—he took a painting down from the wall to uncover a safe hiding behind it.

"You know the saying 'know your enemy?'" Knox said, dig-ging through the safe, finally turning back to us with a single piece of paper. "Well, I take that quite literally. Over the years, I've had a list of every drifter I've come to know about."

"You made a list? Of people?"

"Drifters," Knox corrected, like there was a significant difference. "And unfortunately, someone stole it."

He sat back down, still holding the paper.

"Then what is that?" I asked.

"I keep two copies, because I'm not an idiot. This is the only thing I have that might help you find your parents. If you can find the person taking the drifters, maybe they'll lead you back to your mom and dad."

Knox handed me the list and Reid eyed it, asking, "How is this supposed to help us?"

"Whoever is responsible, they're going down the list one by one, so if you find the next person before they're taken—"

I finished for him. "Then maybe we can stop them."

Knox sat back, nodding. "We would do it ourselves, but we obviously can't travel like you do. You'll need to be fast, try to get to the next person before it's too late."

I gripped the folded list in my hand, wondering how on Earth I could pull this off. Did he know who he was talking to? I had *just* learned to drift. I didn't know what I was doing.

Reid put a hand on my arm and I looked over at him.

He said, "We can do this."

And for some reason, I believed him.

"And to help you guys out," Knox said, "I'm sending my son, Gavin, with you."

Reid stiffened next to me and I immediately shook my head. "That's not necessary."

"No, it's fine," Reid said, and I gave him a confused look. He told me, "We can use all the help we can get."

I took a deep breath and asked Knox, "So this is it? You bring us here, give us a list, and send us on our way?"

His mouth pressed into a thin line and finally said, "I wish I could do more. Please believe me when I say that."

145

I stood, keeping a good grip on the list, like it was the only lifeline I had left. "I'm not going to believe anything until I find my family."

Knox nodded and said, "I really hope you do."

"And in the meantime, the least you can do is fix the door your people broke at my house and make sure my dog is taken care of."

Reid glanced at me like he couldn't believe I was making demands. Honestly, I couldn't believe it, either, but it helped me feel like I had some control. Like I hadn't just been taken against my will.

Knox actually smiled—just the teeniest amount, but still. "It's the least I could do," he agreed.

I glanced at Reid, silently telling him it was time to go, and we both left the room, not looking back. Another pair of footsteps followed us down the hall and out the front door. I didn't like the idea of Gavin going with us, but did we have a choice?

Reid was tense beside me, and once we reached the driveway, he whirled on him. "What the hell, Gavin?"

In turn, Gavin glanced at the house, making sure nobody was around, and he finally said, "Look, I'm sorry, but we always made it a point to never talk about our families."

Wait, what?

"You guys know each other?" I voiced, feeling *really* confused.

Reid scratched the back of his head and gestured at Gavin. "Well, I thought I did, but apparently that was just a misunderstanding. It might've been good to know that your father was *Knox*. The guy who has it out for every drifter around."

Gavin shook his head, practically rolling his eyes. "That's not true and you know it. Buck is worse than him."

"Did you just try to make a joke?" Reid asked.

Gavin threw his arms out and yelled, "What else am I supposed to do? If you knew who my father was, you never would

146

have been friends with me." He took a few breaths and said more quietly, "And I—I couldn't *not* be friends with you."

I glanced at Reid, whose shoulders finally relaxed, and he gave a smiling smirk before saying, "I think you know me well enough to know—I'm not that easy to get rid of."

Gavin shrugged. "I suppose you do need to keep eating."

That's when Reid broke out into an actual smile. "That's not all you're good for."

"I'm sorry I didn't tell you."

"It doesn't matter, I was just . . . surprised."

"I was surprised when you turned up at Sam's house. You're crazy, you know that?"

Reid admitted, "Okay, but my secret wasn't as big as yours." Gavin nodded and Reid finally turned to me. "You ready to find your family?" He pointed a thumb at Gavin. "I think it's okay if this guy tags along."

"As long as you think he can help."

Gavin nodded at the paper. "The sooner we get started, the better."

I studied the folded paper in my hand and then opened it. It was like this was just the first page of a very complicated and thorough project. Like an index. The first column of names was a list of known deceased drifters. The second, a list of possible known drifters. And the third column was a list of confirmed drifters. Knox had circled the third list of names for me already, like it wasn't obvious.

There were a lot of names I didn't recognize, and then there was Mom's name, and under hers was Logan's. Looking at his name, I wondered, *How did it happen?* Maybe he was coming back from class, ready to take a nap for the day, and they came for him while he was sleeping. I hadn't seen any signs of a struggle in his room and his phone was still there.

There were a lot of possibilities, and all of them didn't matter because he was already gone.

"They're both on here," I said, still staring at the list. Would I be on the list if I knew I was a drifter sooner? Would I have already been taken?

Gavin asked, "Who is listed after your brother?"

I pulled my eyes off Logan's name and read the next name. "Someone named Jake Courtney." I looked up at Reid. "Your friend's name is Jake, right? Is that him?"

The look on his face gave me the answer. Reid's gaze unfocused instantly, looking for his friend, and I feared the worst.

"I can't find him," Reid whispered and then he tried again and again.

Whoever these people were, they were finding drifters way too fast. Reid looked visibly nervous, and I didn't know what to do or how to make it better. I took his hand and he squeezed mine back.

Gavin put a hand on Reid's shoulder. "We'll find him. Where does he live? We'll start there."

Reid took a moment to refocus and answered the question. "He's got a few places, but he was in Tokyo earlier tonight, so he's probably staying there."

"Let's go."

Reid glanced at me, worry etched in every corner of his face. "We'll find him," I said.

He took a deep breath, took Gavin's hand in his other, and drifted us away.

REID

TOKYO, JAPAN

I FIRST MET JAKE TWO YEARS BEFORE MY PARENTS died.

When you're young, you like to do things without your parents knowing. Like sneaking out of the house. Going to the movies when you promised you'd be at a friend's house. Sometimes spending money on things they told you not to buy.

So the drifter's equivalent to that was, of course, drifting somewhere when your parents told you to stay home. I decided to check out the Gold Coast in Australia, mostly because I saw it in some movie I watched.

I liked it better when Jake told the story because he always had a good visual of me standing on the beach. He always said, "He was totally out of place, wind still in his hair, the whole deal."

It was true—I was very out of place and definitely not dressed for the beach.

Then I saw this guy coming out of the waves, surfboard under his arm, like some sort of movie scene. I was starstruck, like most kids are when they see someone older than they are, looking cool and doing cool things.

Then Jake asked, "You wanna try to surf?"

I couldn't even believe he was talking to me, let alone offering me his board. I stripped off most of my clothes before he could change his mind. I tried, and failed, and once when I was falling off the board, I accidentally drifted back onto the beach.

All Jake said to me was, "Next time, trying drifting back *on* the surfboard."

It was like he already knew me, inside and out.

And after all this time, I had never bothered staying in his apartment in Tokyo, not even once.

I still remembered the day he showed it to me, all excitement and smiles. He was waiting for me to get excited, too, and was left with only disappointment. After everything that had happened, it was hard for me to find joy, even for him.

After he had taken me on the mini tour of the living area, the kitchen, and the master bedroom, he showed me the guest room. He never actually asked, but I knew what he was doing.

He was saying, *I'll always have room for you.*

How had I been so blind? So . . . ungrateful? Yeah, I didn't like *how* he got the money, but his heart was always in the right place. Yes, I was depressed, but he was always there for me.

He probably cared more than I'll ever know.

I didn't deserve him.

Now he was gone.

Dishes were broken in the kitchen, the TV was smashed, lamps were shattered on the floor, and there was no sign of anyone.

I left Sam and Gavin in the living room to go examine the door, checking for forced entry. Since Jake never actually used the door, he always kept it locked.

It was like nobody had touched it since he first bought the place.

I turned back to the room, something itching in the corner of my thoughts. Sam stood in the living room, piece of paper still in hand, looking a bit lost, and Gavin had wandered off to look in the bedrooms.

I studied the apartment, a certain thought still lingering, one I didn't want to believe was true. There had obviously been a fight in the kitchen, the way everything was broken, and there were drops of blood on the sink.

Another fight had taken place in the living room, particularly in the corner, where the TV was broken, along with a lamp and an overturned chair.

I glanced around the apartment more, searching.

Gavin came out of the master bedroom and, upon seeing my face, he asked, "What is it?"

"Was there anything wrong in the bedroom?"

He shook his head but then said, "Looks like there was a fight in the bathroom, though."

"But nothing in the bedroom?"

Gavin glanced behind, finally shaking his head, shrugging. "Not that I can see. Why?"

I had to make sure, but everything I saw was pointing toward it. I couldn't ignore it.

"Reid?" Sam asked.

For a moment, I didn't say anything, thinking, or maybe hoping, I was wrong. Then I said, "I think another drifter is taking them."

Sam let out a sharp breath and Gavin asked, "Why?"

They waited for me to answer, and I was more certain now that I had said it aloud.

"Because everything in here points to it. There were three

151

separate fights in this apartment, and yet nothing was touched between those areas."

Sam asked, "What if it was just Jake doing the drifting?"

"It's a possibility, but I don't think so. There was no forced entry and all the locks are still in place. And—" I paused, wondering why I hadn't seen it before. Why hadn't *anyone* seen it before? "Who best to find other drifters . . . than another drifter? Think about it. Sliders are good at fighting us, sure, but would they be able to go halfway around the world catching drifters in a matter of days? Drifters are the only ones who can find other drifters . . . one of our own kind could become our worst enemy."

Gavin swore silently and Sam said, "So while everyone thought the sliders were our only enemies, it's actually another drifter?"

"It's the only thing that makes sense, right? Who else could find drifters who were in hiding? Jake has multiple houses around the world, so who else would know he was here at this moment unless they could see him?"

Was I even making any sense? I took a deep breath and sat on the couch. Everything smelled like Jake, like his Tide laundry detergent and the same expensive cologne he's always used, and if I thought about him too hard, my throat tightened. Every moment I didn't take with him suddenly felt like too many.

The view was a good distraction. Jake knew what he wanted in an apartment: expensive furniture and a good view.

Sam sat down next to me and said, "I think you're right."

Gavin came over, righting the toppled chair across from us, and took a seat. "So do I," he said, leaning his elbows on his knees.

It was weird having him there—but in a good way. I wouldn't have known what to do if he wasn't.

I said, "So what do we do about it?"

Sam answered, smiling, "If it's one drifter, they're already outnumbered. Let's just focus on finding them first."

I didn't know how she was staying so calm—her whole family was missing. And there I was, missing one friend and I was on the brink of a breakdown.

But with Gavin and Sam sitting there with me, I wasn't alone.

Even though I could be anywhere in the world, I was content being there with them, sitting in Jake's broken living room and trying to be helpful. So many years I avoided being in this world full of people like me because it always reminded me too much of my family.

But sometimes family isn't blood. Sometimes it's your brother from another country, just trying to make you feel like you belonged.

I cleared my throat and asked, "What's the next name on the list?"

Sam unfolded the paper and I leaned over to look at the names. I saw mine right away, not too far down from Jake's, and she glanced over at me, like she'd already seen it and didn't want to tell me.

Sam said, "The next person is Sabrina Cortés."

"I've met her," I told them. "A few days ago, she was talking to Jake. They were trying to figure out who was behind all this when they thought it was still the sliders."

"Can you find her?"

I quickly did and said, "She's in Venezuela, near the coast."

Gavin stood. "Then let's go before it's too late."

SAM

CHIRIMENA, VENEZUELA

GOING FROM NIGHT, TO MORNING, TO NIGHT again was a bit disconcerting. I'd never been to a jungle before, obviously, and there I was, in a jungle in the middle of the night, listening to animal sounds I didn't recognize and the swell of the ocean not too far off.

There was a small house in front of us, the windows glowing softly with light, and Reid was already heading toward it. Gavin gave me this look that said, *I guess we should follow him.* So we did.

Reid knocked on the door and a voice yelled from inside. "This is private property!"

He yelled back, "It's Reid! Jake's friend!"

There was a pause, footsteps, and then the door opened. The woman was really pretty and had very fierce-looking eyes, like she'd punch someone if the moment called for it.

"Yeah, I remember you," Sabrina said. "What are you doing here?"

She glanced over at me and Gavin, but when Reid said, "Jake was taken," her eyes snapped back to him.

"How do you know?"

"Because I can't find him and his apartment was trashed."

There was a long moment of silence as she took us all in, probably wondering if this was some sort of joke. But when her eyes finally settled on Reid, her mind was mind up.

Sabrina stepped outside, now looking more worried than a moment ago. She folded her arms across her chest like she had gotten a sudden chill, but it wasn't cold. It was actually *really* warm, and I was wearing a jacket I wanted to take off.

"So he's really gone? Like the others?" Sabrina asked.

"Yeah, but that's not all," Reid said. "I think another drifter is the one taking them."

Sabrina only seemed partially surprised to hear it, and she actually nodded. "We were starting to suspect but didn't have any proof. So what are you doing *here*? If another drifter is coming, you'd better make more slider friends like that one," she said, nodding to Gavin. "Before it's too late."

She actually started to turn away, but Reid said, "We have reason believe they'll be coming for you next. We came to warn you."

She had very little reaction to that and shrugged. "And then?"

I finally spoke up, "We're trying to help you and you're acting like none of this matters."

Sabrina's eyes slid to mine, more callous than before.

"Does it? We tried to fix this before and look where it got us." She dipped her head a moment and took a breath. "Look, I'm sorry. It's just . . . I'm not sure how anyone can help at this point. *We* haven't even found out where they're being taken or who is taking them. I doubt three teenagers can do it."

Gavin grumbled, "Ouch."

"But at least we're *trying*," Reid said.

Sabrina let the door slam behind her and took a step closer.

"And where were you when Jake asked for help before? It seems to me you're only interested now that Jake is gone."

I didn't have to see his face to know her words hit him hard.

"Maybe," he admitted. "But now that I've started, I won't be giving up."

"This might take you a few years to understand, but sometimes giving up means staying alive."

"But what is it worth? Your friends? Your f—" Reid stopped like he wasn't sure he wanted to say it. He finally whispered, "Your family?"

Sabrina said, "Everyone has to make their own decisions and live with that. They're your choices . . . nobody else's. It's up to me what I can live with."

"So you're fine just giving up and hiding away in this cabin until you have no more friends or family left? I'm sure they're on the list somewhere. You're okay with doing nothing?"

"Maybe."

"That's not an answer."

"And I don't have to give you one!"

I was afraid I would actually see Sabrina punch him, but then something whispered into my ear, a sound I'd come to know and love. I glanced around and saw nothing but dark jungle.

"Stop," I said, searching the dark. Something in my voice must have tipped them off because they actually did. Shadows moved under the trees, and the wind was too loud, rustling the branches, to hear anything else. But I knew what I had heard. It couldn't have been anything else.

I said, "I think they're here."

Everyone stood silent, listening. I stepped off the porch and closer to the trees where I thought I'd heard it.

Someone stepped out of the shadows.

It was a guy, maybe in his mid-twenties, and he didn't look

like some villain who was taking people. He just looked . . . normal. Except for the gun in his hand—not normal.

Sabrina's voice echoed from behind. *"Kiato? What are you doing here?"*

Kiato glanced at us and then Sabrina and then he said, "I'm sorry."

He raised the gun at someone over my shoulder and pulled the trigger before I could react, but instead of a loud gunshot, it was a soft, almost muted sound.

I looked behind me, and Gavin was already a blur coming toward us. Then he was less a blur and more of a fuzzy figure, then he was just himself, staggering. He looked down to the red tranquilizer dart in his shoulder.

I let out a breath. "Gavin."

I caught him by the arm as he dropped to a knee, his gaze already becoming unfocused.

"Kiato, please don't do this," Sabrina called to him. "Whatever it is, whatever is happening with you—"

"Nothing you say can change this," he said. "I have my orders."

"Orders from who?" Sabrina asked, half desperate. "What do they want with any of us? What do they want with *me*?"

Then Kiato paused and said, "I'm not here for you."

He looked at Reid and my breath caught again, not knowing what I should do.

Kiato put away his gun and drifted. Reid was quick, drifting away before Kiato could touch him. Next, they were in a standoff with each other. I remembered watching Reid at the fight club, but that was against a normal person. How would he do against another drifter?

Kiato came at him and Reid sidestepped, but Kiato was ready for him this time. Both of them disappeared in the scuffle and then reappeared again next to the forest edge, throwing punches. They drifted again, appearing in the middle of the clearing, their fight never stopping.

Gavin slouched farther to the ground and I let him, more worried about Reid because Gavin wasn't in the same amount of trouble.

Making sure Gavin was safely on the ground, I stood, watching Reid and Kiato fight it out. When I saw a good opportunity, I drifted behind Kiato and grabbed the back of his jacket to pull him off Reid. He stumbled backward and glared at me, both surprised and mad about the interruption.

"Sam."

I looked at Reid, at the small cut above his eye, at the corners of his mouth that I was waiting to turn up into a smile. Between the both of us, we could do it—we could beat him together and find out where my family was.

I could see it all lining up perfectly.

The air changed over Reid's shoulder and Kiato appeared behind him, grabbing him from behind. And before I could reach out for him or help . . . they were gone.

They didn't reappear.

Gavin finally woke up when the sun was just starting to rise. Sabrina only had one bed—which we put Gavin on—and then she let me stay on her couch. And even though I didn't think I would be able to sleep after everything that happened, I did.

Gavin and I were drinking black coffee at the table when Sabrina joined us, smelling like sand and salt after talking a walk on the beach.

"I thought you would have left by now," Gavin said to her.

"We may have gone into hiding, but we aren't cowards.

And what's the point of leaving if he's not after me? And it's not like I can hide anyway."

I said, "The list was wrong, then."

The list was wrong and Reid was taken, and not even someone as skilled as Sabrina could find him. It could only mean one thing—he was with the others. He had to be; I didn't believe they were all dead. Why would they bother taking them if they were just going to kill them?

Gavin said the only thing on my mind. "So how do we find them?"

I had no answers, and Sabrina just shook her head. How were we going to find them without any idea where to look?

"Who's this Kiato guy?" Gavin asked Sabrina.

"I knew his sister through a friend. I have no idea what he's gotten himself into, but I know he's not a bad person. I never would have imagined it was him doing all this."

"So this sister, can you find her?"

Sabrina's eyes unfocused and she immediately swore, slamming the table with a fist. "It's the same as the others—nothing."

"There's got to be something else we can do. We need another piece of information. There has to be something we're missing," Gavin said.

I thought about Knox and how he and Dad used to be friends. Did Dad have any idea what was happening? Were they actually going on a trip for their anniversary, or was it all a cover-up for trying to figure out who was taking drifters? How many people were trying to figure this out before they had disappeared one by one?

"I'm going to go home," I announced, and before Gavin could freak out, I continued, "My parents have a study there, and maybe they left behind some clues to where they were going last weekend because I doubt they were actually taking a vacation with all of this happening. Maybe we could retrace their steps."

Gavin thought about it. "It's a place to start at least."

"While you guys do that," Sabrina said, "I'm going to track down the rest of Kiato's family and see if I can find anything useful. It might be a dead end, but . . ."

I wondered if she was thinking about what Reid had said to her last night, about not giving up.

It was a half-formed plan riding on hope, but at least it was better than what we had this morning. It was *something*.

REID

I'D BEEN IN A LOT OF FIGHTS BEFORE, BUT NOTH-ing like this.

While I was distracted by Sam—a very good distraction, don't get me wrong—Kiato grabbed me from behind and then we were in a field somewhere in Colombia. He was trying to get my arms behind my back, and I elbowed him in the ribs.

I took him to a roof in Rome, getting the upper hand. I got a good hit on his jaw and then he tackled me and we appeared in a busy street in Beijing. A trolley stopped inches from us as we fought in the road, and cars honked.

Before anyone could pull out their cell phones, we were gone again.

A mountainside in Slovenia.

An empty beach in California.

A farm in Russia.

All within minutes. Getting pushed into walls, throwing punches, and almost being hit in the head with a pipe he'd managed to grab somewhere.

And then I was falling, like jumping from an airplane

without a parachute. I'd never drifted so high up in the sky before—I didn't even think it was possible. Wind roared in my ears and my stomach fell out from under me as I plummeted toward the ground.

Kiato was nowhere in sight, but he was the one who had brought me there.

Then something caught my eye to the right, coming from above.

I turned just in time to get knocked out.

When I came to, I was being dragged by the ankle. Everything was still hazy and my head wouldn't stop spinning. Nausea flared in my stomach. A light flashed above and then it was dark, then another light, and more dark. It was hard to keep my eyes open.

There was a snap of a chain somewhere close.

"Reid!"

I tried to open my eyes more, to see where he was. It was Jake. I didn't imagine it. I tried to twist away, to grab onto something, but Kiato pulled me closer to a wall and dropped my leg. A groan escaped my mouth and I knew I needed to get out of there. I needed to drift. But how could I drift when I could barely lift my head?

I'd never taken a hit so hard in my life.

"Reid!"

Jake's voice was a little farther away now, muffled by a wall. There was movement above me and my eyes focused enough to see Kiato standing over me.

I needed to get out of there.

I thought of the first place that came to mind and drifted. My body snapped back into place and my shoulder

162

screamed with pain, like I had almost dislocated it. I was still in the same place as Kiato looked down at me. I tried again and the same thing happened.

"It's not going to work," Kiato said in a tired voice.

I looked over at my wrist. There was a metal cuff around it, attached to a chain that was bolted into the cement floor.

"What did you do?" I said, my voice rough and cracking.

I pushed myself up and my head spun too fast, almost making me want to puke. I could feel the threads of panic starting to set in. Was he going to leave me here? And where was Jake? I swore I had heard his voice, but there were walls blocking my view and I could only see the open, empty room of an old warehouse. I was in something like a cement stall, walls six feet wide on both sides and too high for me to see over.

They didn't need cells or bars to keep us here.

They just needed us to be bolted. Chained like animals.

Kiato started to walk away.

"Wait!" I reached for him and the chain stopped me short. He kept going, leaving me.

I swore under my breath and looked around, trying to figure out where we were. The location didn't come to mind—like when I was trying to find Jake. It was like it didn't exist. The ceiling was high and covered in glass panels that showed the night sky. That fact narrowed down half the world.

But there was sound—a buzzing. Really low and barely audible, coming from this cylindrical speaker on the ceiling with tons of wires hooked up into it.

"Found it already, huh?" Buck appeared around the corner, smiling down at me. "It took years to figure out the right frequency, but now I've found out how to keep your friends from finding you."

I looked up at it again. This was what blocked me from seeing Jake? Something so simple as a frequency?

"So Knox lied," I said. "He really *was* taking drifters."

"Don't dismiss me so quickly, Reid. Knox has no idea I was the one who stole his list and he has no idea I'm doing *any* of this."

"Why *are* you doing this?" I asked him. "What have we ever done to you?"

Buck moved so quickly, I never saw him coming. One second he was standing at the corner of my cell, and the next he was pressing me against the wall, one hand fisted in my jacket and the other wrapped around my throat.

I couldn't breathe. The cuff around my wrist strained against the chain, drawing blood. He loosened his grip just enough to let me breathe.

"When I was young, my father took me to a diner for lunch and this man showed up while we were eating. They went into the bathroom to talk and when I followed a minute later, they were both gone. They didn't come out the door and there were no windows. Nothing. They just disappeared." Buck paused and clenched his jaw a few times. "A couple days later, a fishing boat found his body off the coast of Japan. Everyone said it was a boating accident and I believed it until I found out about drifters. Then all the pieces came together. A drifter took my father and left him for dead in the middle of the ocean."

Buck shook his head, tightening his grip. "That's only one of many stories I could tell you, Reid. Your kind acts like you're so *entitled* with this great power that none of you deserve. And there's only *us* to stop you."

Jake's voice echoed from down the hall, desperate and angry. "Let him go, Buck!"

Buck continued, not listening.

"So it's about time someone did something about it."

The corners of my vision swam dark and he finally let go, dropping me to the floor. I coughed and tried to breathe. Buck started walking away.

"So that's it?" I coughed out. "You're going to keep us here until we die?"

Buck stopped and turned back, shaking his head. "What good would that do? I found someone who is very interested in people with special abilities, and he even has his own lab dedicated to working on a way to harness them. So we struck a deal, and I get to find him drifters to do his testing on."

"So this is just a job?"

"Enough to set me up for life," Buck said, spreading his arms. "And getting rid of a few drifters in the process? That's just a bonus." Buck glanced at my wrist and the blood on the cuff. "Don't worry, we have one more drifter to find and then it'll be over." He smiled. "Not much longer now."

"Who? Who are you sending him after?"

Even though I asked, I knew the answer.

"We can't leave behind any loose ends."

With that, Buck left. His footsteps echoed through the room until a door shut, leaving me alone with the dull buzzing overhead. Someone coughed down from the other direction and I wondered how many drifters he was keeping here, and how many of them were dying because their bodies were already shutting down.

It was cold with all the cement around and I was glad for my jacket. My head still hurt from being knocked out and I touched the place gently, feeling drying blood on my temple.

"Reid." It was Jake. From the sound of his voice, I could tell that he was probably two stalls away. "Are you okay?"

"Yeah."

But it was a lie.

Sam and Gavin were our only hope now.

SAM

NEW YORK, UNITED STATES

KNOX WAS GOOD TO HIS WORD AND HAD FIXED our back door, and when Gavin and I showed up, Levi was waiting for me in the kitchen, wagging his tail too fast. It felt good to be home again, but only for a moment, because I realized nobody else was there.

Then a glass shattered in the hallway, making me jump.

Nella stood there, shock written all over her face.

She screamed and then screamed again when she realized a strange guy was standing next to me.

"Nella! It's okay, it's okay!" I walked toward her with my hands up. She stopped screaming, looking between Gavin and me like she had no idea what she had just seen.

I realized that this was the reaction Reid had expected from me when he showed me drifting for the first time. It was totally understandable.

She was breathing too quickly and looked like she wanted to scream again. I put my hands on her shoulders and that seemed to calm her down some. She kept glancing over my shoulder, where Gavin stood in the kitchen.

"Nella, look at me."

She did, finally saying. "Sam, you—you . . . what just happened?"

"I know it's a lot to take in. Just one thing at a time, okay?"

She nodded. "Yeah, okay."

I stepped aside and gestured toward the kitchen. "This is Gavin. He's a friend of Reid's."

"Reid," Nella repeated. "Right."

Gavin took the opportunity and said, "I'm going to start in your parents' office. Is it upstairs?"

I nodded, and after he passed us in the hallway—stepping over the broken glass—I led Nella into the kitchen and put her on one of the chairs. I gave her a moment to process what she had seen and I cleaned up the glass. By the time it was safely in the trash and the broom was put away, she looked almost normal. Nervous about something for sure, but better than before.

It was an upgrade from the screaming.

I sat down across from her and said, "Look, I know what you saw was . . . shocking, but there's nothing to be afraid of."

She eyed me like I had just told the biggest lie. "You literally appeared out of thin air, Sam."

"Yeah, like I said . . . shocking." That finally pulled a smile from her and I asked, "What are you doing here, anyway?"

"You weren't answering my texts so I decided to stop by before school started. Everything just seemed—off. Nobody was here and I hadn't heard from you. And even though we had a fight, you always text me back."

"I'm sorry, my phone was broken."

She eyed me and I knew what questions were coming. "What happened, Sam?"

I took a deep breath, wondering what I should tell her or if I should tell her anything. But I didn't want to lie to Nella—she was still my best friend.

So I told her everything. Definitely a shortened version, but I hit all the important parts. I thought she wouldn't believe anything I said, but then she started asking questions when I missed something or if she needed clarification.

"So now that Reid is gone, it's just you and Gavin left?" Nella asked. "There's nobody else helping you?"

"We have someone else helping, but she's following another lead."

"Can't you go to the police?" I gave her a blank look and she realized what that would mean. "All right, yeah. But this is a lot to take in."

I hesitated and said, "I know."

"Are you handling it all? You seem so . . . *calm*."

How *was* I handling it? That was a question I wasn't sure I knew how to answer. When I found out Mom, Dad, and Logan were taken, I'd never felt so alone in my life. Even when Reid was there for me. But since then, it'd been different.

"I don't know," I told her, and it was the truth. "At first it was a lot to take in. But every day that passes makes me feel like I'm less alone. Like I've finally found my place in the world. Does that make sense? And even though it's really messy right now, I know I can help try to fix it. It's . . . part of me now."

Nella was smiling the same way she did when she thought something was super-cute, and I rolled my eyes at her.

"Way to make it into a joke," I accused her.

"No!" She fixed her face. "I'm sorry, I didn't mean it like that, I promise. It's just . . . I'm happy for you."

I nodded, trying to smile. "Okay."

"Okay."

Gavin came downstairs, already talking. "I didn't find anything useful, Sam. If you want to take a look, you can, but—"

As Gavin stepped on the bottom floor, someone appeared in the hallway between us. It was Kiato. He looked at me first and then back to Gavin. My heart rate spiked and I froze, not knowing what to do. We should have expected him to show up at any time, but now that it was happening, I didn't have a plan.

Gavin looked at me and yelled, "Sam, get out of here!"

Knowing Gavin was the bigger threat, Kiato went for him first. He drifted and Gavin slowed time. They danced around each other in the foyer until one of them got slammed against the wall. Since both of them were a blur, I didn't even know who it was.

Levi had his ears flat and a low growl came from his throat. He stayed near me, though, too young to know what to do.

Nella looked like she might scream again, and I quickly grabbed her wrist, drifting us both out of there before it was too late. When we appeared in her bedroom, she looked like she was going to be sick and ran for the bathroom.

I gave her a few seconds after the vomiting stopped and asked, "Are you okay?"

Nella came out of the bathroom, looking gray.

She said, "Please don't do that again."

I put my hands on her arms, looking serious. "I've got to go, okay? Promise me you won't go to my house again until you hear from me."

After a worried hesitation, she finally nodded. "I promise." I started to pull away, but she caught my arm. "Please, Sam—be careful."

"I will," I promised. Before I drifted back home, I told her, "Maybe close your eyes? It might help with the shock."

She gave me a sheepish smile but did it.

I drifted back into the kitchen, completely expecting a full-on fight to be happening in my house.

It was quiet. Like nobody was there at all. Levi wouldn't stop staring at the hallway and finally let out a whine, like he didn't know what to do.

"Gavin?"

Nothing.

Then Kiato appeared again in the same place in the hallway, a big gash over his eye. Gavin wasn't with him. He started coming toward me and Levi started growling, staying near my side. It was all happening too fast. I needed time to think about what to do.

I needed everything to just *slow down* for one damned second.

It was hard to understand what happened then, because I'd never experienced it before.

Like a snap of a finger, everything became muted and Kiato stopped walking—he didn't *stop* walking, but he was moving so slow that I thought he had at first. Then I thought—what was happening? Did *I* do this?

I glanced around to see if Gavin was here somewhere, but it was just Kiato and me.

Kiato.

He was in the kitchen now, still coming for me, even if it was slower than before. If I let him get close enough, it would be over. I needed to go. I needed to drift.

But when I tried—something wasn't right. Kiato was almost an arm's reach from me and when I tried to drift, I didn't go anywhere. Not that nothing happened because *something* definitely did, but I didn't drift away. Instead, the pressure inside my head intensified and something appeared next to me.

There was a tear in the air, like a ripped piece of fabric big enough to fit a person. A seam, with threads of air reaching out as if there was no gravity. I could see the other side of the room through it, but it was blurry, like looking through frosted glass.

It was beautiful.

The moment the seam appeared, time snapped back to

normal, and Kiato stopped short, looking at the crack—or whatever it was—next to me.

I felt just as shocked as he looked.

A pressure pulsed at the back of my head, stronger than ever, and I wasn't sure if I could hold onto it much longer.

I released the pressure and the seam disappeared.

When I looked over at Kiato, he was gone, too.

REID

BEING A DRIFTER MEANT GOING ANYWHERE IN the world I wanted, whenever I wanted. There was nothing to stop me and nothing to hold me back. There were no restrictions about anything, no boundaries I couldn't cross.

I never knew it could be taken away so quickly. And never before had I cherished it so much.

Time seemed to pass slowly wherever we were. I was able to sleep on and off, but couldn't find a comfortable position and my head still swam. I was grateful for my jacket and wondered if anyone else had one.

A few times in the night, I heard groans from down the hall, followed by a snap of a chain as someone tried to drift. They probably couldn't help themselves, and I knew I was listening to my future if this wasn't over soon. Our bodies would start shutting down fast, and out of instinct to save ourselves, we wouldn't have a choice.

I'd never been bolted before. Even though Buck always threatened me with it. But I'd heard stories—all drifters had—of drifters and sliders who hated each other more than most.

Everyone knew—if we didn't drift, we'd die.

Drifting was a part of me as much as my heart, keeping me alive. Without it, I was nothing. Without it, I didn't know who I was.

When morning came, the space we were kept in was actually well-lit because of all the skylights on the ceiling. Jake muttered a sarcastic *good morning* at some point and then Buck came around with a couple other guards who gave us a breakfast that consisted of a bottle of water and a cereal bar.

"I have to go to the bathroom," I told him.

He smiled. "I'll get you the bucket."

Kiato showed up then—literally right behind Buck, who couldn't help but flinch. But Kiato was freaked out about something and lowered his voice. I could still hear him.

"I went to find the girl and something—*happened*."

Buck turned his back on me and asked, "What do you mean 'something happened'?"

Kiato hesitated, eyes darting around. "I'm not quite sure. She . . . *did* something. Something I've never seen before."

Buck held up his hand and said, "I don't care what it is. The buyers are coming tomorrow morning, and I need one more body. Find her and bring her here." Buck leaned in closer and said, "Whatever it takes."

Buck walked away with his guards and Kiato glanced at me.

I took the moment and asked, "Why are you doing this?" He eyed the direction Buck had left in, like he was worried about something or knew he shouldn't be talking to me. Maybe he was scared. I decided to tweak my question. "What does he have on you?"

He finally settled his gaze on me. "He has my sister."

It wasn't something I expected to hear. Buck was keeping his sister here somewhere so he could have leverage to get

173

Kiato to do what he wanted? The best person to find a drifter was another drifter. I guess Buck figured that out way before any of us. But to kidnap someone and use her as blackmail? What kind of person does that? I guess the same type of person keeping drifters locked up long enough to *sell* us.

I swore and Kiato turned to walk away. I couldn't let that happen.

"No, wait. Please."

He turned his head just enough to look at me, uncommitted.

"I can't release you."

"That's not what I want."

That got his attention, or at least his curiosity. I stood; the chain was just long enough to let me.

"The girl you're after. Sam," I told him. "If you give her a chance, she can help us."

"I don't think anyone can help us now."

"Please, just . . . give her some time. I promise, we can help you and your sister. This doesn't have to happen. Not like this."

His face never changed, so I wasn't sure if I was getting to him or not. I hoped I was. Sam and Gavin were smart; they could figure something out. They just needed some time.

Kiato eyed me a moment longer and then drifted away, leaving behind nothing but a breeze.

Seeing him drift while I couldn't sent a wave of nausea through my stomach. I slumped against the wall and the sensation passed. A hint of what was to come.

Jake's muffled voice carried over. "It was worth a try, anyway."

I pressed my face against the cement, feeling hot, and wished I was anywhere else. On any normal day, I would have been.

SAM
WESTERN SAHARA

THE FIRST THING I HAD TO DO WAS FIND GAVIN. I didn't have time to think about what had happened in the kitchen; I just needed to find the only ally I had left. And maybe if I stayed near a slider, Kiato would be more hesitant to come for me again.

I tried to find him, and for a moment, I didn't think it would work. But then I got a picture of him and drifted before I lost it.

The moment I appeared, Gavin let out a sound of relief. He looked like he wanted to hug me, and I couldn't believe it actually worked. I had drifted to him.

"Sam, are you okay? What happened? I was worried that—" He looked around us, at the never-ending desert, and he took a shattering breath. Gavin didn't need to finish that sentence for me to know.

He was worried that I had been taken, and he would be stuck here until he died.

"I'm okay," I said.

Gavin sat down on the sand and ran his shaking hands through his hair, looking defeated and a little relieved.

He said, "Growing up a slider, you learn one thing over and over again: never let a drifter leave you some place you don't want to be."

I sat down beside him and it felt good, just being there, sitting and not running from someone. The warm breeze threaded between us, and the sun was orange on the horizon, deep in the afternoon. The sand was warm but not too hot to sit on now that the day was coming to an end here.

"I don't know what happened," he said. "When I'm in that kind of fight, I plan my moves at least three in advance because it only takes a second for a mistake to happen. One second we were here, and I thought I had a good hold on him, but . . . he was just gone. It was the first thing my dad ever taught me— never let go. I messed up, bad."

Reid and Gavin grew up in opposite worlds, learning the dangers from either side. Now that I'd seen a little of both, they were more similar than they thought. Different but still the same.

"How did you and Reid become friends?" I asked, curious.

Gavin thought about it, looking a little less stressed now that he wasn't stuck here. "I think we just realized we weren't enemies, no matter how long we'd been taught we were supposed to be."

"Maybe times are changing," I said, and he looked over at me. "I mean, look at us. We're supposed to be enemies, too, but your dad was the one who sent you with us."

Gavin finally gave a nod and looked back at the horizon. "I hope you're right."

I thought back to what happened in the kitchen, and maybe Gavin was the perfect person to ask. My heart kicked too fast a couple times and then I just decided to go for it.

"So when you mess with time, does everything become muted and you get this pressure inside your head?"

Gavin snapped his head around. "What?" he yelled, stunned. "How—what are you talking about?"

"Something happened," I started. "When Kiato came back to the house for me, I think I did . . . whatever you do. I slowed down time."

Gavin opened his mouth, but it was like his brain didn't compute what I was saying. In his eyes, I was a drifter. Nothing else.

"Your dad . . ." he said, searching me. "I don't think a drifter and a slider have ever been together before, so this is like, uncharted territory. That we know of, anyway." Gavin paused and whispered, "Do you have both of their abilities, Sam?"

I nodded, unable to say it.

Gavin swore, looking away. But not the angry kind of swearing, the kind of swearing that meant *wow*.

"That's not all . . ."

He swung around again, this time looking weary. "What do you mean, that's not all?"

How was I going to explain this? *I* didn't even know what happened.

"When I was slowing time, I tried to drift. But then something *happened*."

Gavin raised an eyebrow. "*What* happened?"

I paused, not sure how to explain it.

"It was like a tear in the air, a crack. The pressure in my head got even worse, like I was doing something wrong, but as long as I held it, it was there. When I let go, it disappeared."

Gavin looked away and took a deep breath.

"Have you ever heard of anything like that?" I asked him.

"No, but like I said—uncharted territory." Gavin hesitated. "Do you think you could do it again? Just so I could see?"

I shook my head. "I don't know. I don't even know how I did it the first time."

"You said you were slowing time and then you tried to drift. So doing both things must have messed with something. Like a reaction."

I gave a nervous laugh. "Then I should be lucky I didn't explode?"

Gavin half-heartedly nodded. "Yeah."

"Okay," I said, tentatively, "but I'm not sure I can do it again."

"Do you want to try?"

No, I didn't want to try, because I was afraid it wouldn't work. But I was also afraid it *would* work and something worse would happen. I couldn't help but wonder if I was messing with something I shouldn't.

I stood in front of Gavin and he looked like he was waiting for me to do a magic trick. A magic trick that might explode.

"Just don't overthink it," he said, reminding me of Reid when he first told me how to drift. "Just feel it."

Reid. Even though we barely knew each other, I missed him. I missed his face and the way he filled the empty space beside me. The way he smiled when he thought something was funny and the way he smiled when he thought something was amazing. The way he never gave up.

I wasn't sure if this could help save him, but if there was a chance, I had to take it.

I could do this, for him, for my family. Just a few days ago, I knew nothing about this world full of people with abilities, and then I found out the people who were part of it were just as special as the magic inside them. I could do this.

To make it easier, I closed my eyes and thought about being in the kitchen when Kiato was coming at me. The moment I needed everything to slow down. What it felt like. *How* it felt.

Just like drifting, it came as easy as breathing, like it had always been a part of me, waiting to be let out.

The sounds of the wind became muted and I opened my eyes to see Gavin looking up at me expectantly, like a video in slow motion. Now I just needed to think of a place to drift. Once I had it in mind, I made like I was going to go but the same thing happened again.

Instead of drifting, the pressure in my head pulsed brighter and the seam appeared, holding tendrils of the air we always left behind when we drifted.

The moment it happened, time returned to normal and Gavin stood up in a rush, staring at the crack.

When I looked at it again, a thought, almost unbelievable, passed through me. But the hope of it being true was too strong to ignore.

If I was right, it could change everything.

"I want you to try to go through it, Gavin." My voice sounded almost desperate, and I realized it was because my head was starting to hurt. I needed him to hurry.

He peeled his eyes off the crack in the air to look at me, eyebrows raised. "You want me to do *what now*?"

The pressure was almost too much and my heart was beating fast, like my body knew I was almost at my limit. I wasn't sure how long I could hold it open.

"You just have to trust me," I told him.

Gavin stepped closer to the portal and reached his hand toward it, like he was afraid of being burned. When he brushed his fingers against it and nothing happened, he glanced at me, and then he reached in farther. His whole arm went through, and when he brought it back out again, it was still intact.

Gavin told me, "You better be right about this."

"Hurry," I whispered, sweat beading on my brow.

The pressure was building more now and my knees were about to buckle, like I was holding a weight on my shoulders.

Gavin stepped through, right foot first, then his right arm and shoulder. He glanced at me once more and then he was gone.

I released the pressure with a gasp and it disappeared, leaving me alone in the desert. I dropped to my knees in the hot sand, breathing heavily. My head swam even though the pain was gone, and my heart was still pounding too hard.

A plan was already forming in my mind, and for the first time since my family was taken, I felt hopeful. Like maybe we could pull this off.

But first, I needed to ask someone for help.

I drifted to Gavin's driveway a minute later and he whipped around, already grinning. It worked. He was standing in the place I had envisioned when the seam appeared.

"Sam, that was . . . *amazing.* How did you know I could go through it?"

"I didn't," I admitted, "but I had a feeling. After you stepped through it, was it still there?"

"Yeah, but just for a second."

There were two black SUVs sitting in the driveway, and I glanced at the house, wondering if Knox was here. I said, "We need to talk to your dad."

Gavin's smile turned down. "Why?"

"Because I don't think we can do this without him."

He looked weary at the thought of it but finally nodded and led me into the house. We passed his sister in the hallway and she barely looked up from her phone before telling Gavin that Knox was on the back patio. Gavin led me through the kitchen and outside where there was a pool closed for the season.

Knox was sitting at a table on the other side, drinking a cup of coffee with a laptop open in front of him.

He glanced up as we walked over, assessing us like he was trying to figure out why we were here.

"Did you find them?" Knox asked.

I stepped in front of Gavin and said, "We need your help."

His lips pressed together, and he sat back into his chair. "I already gave you help by giving you the list. I'm not sure what else I can do—or *want* to do."

My plan wasn't going to work without him, and I needed to convince him of that without looking desperate. I needed to remind him why I was there in the first place.

Without asking, I sat down across from him, slapping the list on the table.

"The list is useless now," I said, pushing it toward him. "They aren't going in order and, if my assumptions are right, they'll probably be coming for me next."

Gavin made an unhappy sound behind me, and Knox narrowed his eyes. "So what *have* you figured out? Do you know where they're being taken? Do you know who is taking them?"

"It's a drifter," I said, "but I don't think he's behind it. I think whoever *is*, is using him."

"Then why are you here and what do you think I can do about it?"

I glanced behind at Gavin, knowing there was a better chance at Knox believing my story since Gavin had just experienced it firsthand. So I explained it again and when I was done, Knox just laughed.

"That's the most ridiculous thing I've ever heard," he said.

Gavin told him, "It's true. I just walked through it to get here."

181

Knox paused, looking between us. He must have known Gavin wasn't lying to him—what reason would he have?

"And?" he asked me. "I'm assuming you came here with a plan?"

I swallowed, suddenly doubting everything about it.

Reid wouldn't doubt it—so I tried not to either as I told Knox what I had in mind. Hearing the words come out of my mouth, I knew they sounded crazy, like in what universe would this normally be possible? But for me, none of this was possible a week ago, so I guessed anything could happen now.

When I was finished, Knox pushed back his chair and stood, not saying a word. He went over to the edge of the pool, and there was a long moment of silence as he stood there, facing away from us.

"How long have you known my dad?" I'm not sure what made me ask.

He didn't turn. "Since we were about your age."

I stood and went over to him. After a moment, he took a side glance at me and met my eyes.

"You stopped keeping in touch after he met my mom, right?" It was only a guess, but when his eyes narrowed, I knew I was right. I continued, "I know you have your differences, but if he were here, in your situation, he wouldn't hesitate to help you. We're all in this together."

My heart pounded as he stared back at me, wondering if I had said the right words to convince him.

"She's right, Dad," Gavin said behind me. "We need to help them."

Knox turned to his son and asked, "And why are you so sympathetic toward drifters all of a sudden?"

Gavin glanced at me and I knew what he was about to give up. What he was risking.

"The drifter that came here with Sam," he said, taking a

deep breath, "Reid? We've been friends for years, and I never told you because I was worried—" Gavin stopped there, like he didn't know what words to say. "I was worried you'd hate me for it. And for what? Being friends with a drifter?"

"You don't know what you're talking about—"

"But I do," Gavin said quickly. "You might think I don't pay attention to what goes on around here, but I *do*. I know some drifters aren't good—I get that. Not all sliders are good either. The same goes with everyone else in the world. But that doesn't mean they're all like that."

"Gavin—"

"This is our chance to help them, and I'm not going to turn my back on them."

Knox let out a breath, looking between us.

"This will be dangerous for you," he told me. "You'll be exposing yourself."

"I don't care."

Knox rubbed his hand down his face and looked away. The wind picked up a little, sending some of the last leaves down from the trees.

"You remind me a lot of your dad," Knox finally said. "He can be so stubborn. He never gives up."

I didn't say anything, holding my breath.

Knox turned to us and said, "Let's do this."

SAM

NEW YORK, UNITED STATES

I MADE SURE TO HAVE AT LEAST TWO SLIDERS with me while everyone was getting ready, and Knox was hashing out the details about what was going to happen. I'd thought some of the other sliders would have been hesitant about helping the drifters—just like Knox had been—but they were actually eager to help.

Knox kept trying to get a hold of one of his men—Buck—but he wasn't answering, along with a few others that were close to him. He seemed concerned about it, but acted like it wasn't a big deal.

Sabrina showed up, weary to be around so many sliders, but unfortunately, she didn't come with any news. Kiato's family hadn't seen him, or his sister, in a couple weeks. Besides that, we knew nothing.

Gavin's mom fed everyone lunch and she thrived in kitchen. It was easy to tell she loved having so many people there to entertain. It was my worst nightmare. I wanted to find a corner to hide in. Adventure had never been my thing. Give me a puzzle and an anime show and let me be.

But I refrained, knowing the safest place for me was in a room full of sliders.

Kiato never showed up and now, when I really needed him to, he was nowhere to be found.

Hours later, I sat at my kitchen table, rubbing Levi behind his ears.

We would have had family dinner tonight, and it was Dad's turn to cook. He always made the best meals, and it was suddenly really hard sitting at the table without them there. I could see the family pictures on the refrigerator and I could smell the scented candle Mom loved to burn next to the sink.

I just had to remind myself—everything would be back to normal tomorrow.

I heard the sound then and felt the soft breeze.

I let out a sigh of relief.

Levi put his ears back, but I called him off and stood, facing Kiato. I hadn't noticed before, but there were dark circles under his eyes and his skin was too pale.

"Was he right?" he asked, staying where he was. "Did you have enough time?"

At first, I wasn't sure what he was talking about, but the desperate tone of his voice helped me figure it out. Reid must have talked to him and tried to convince him to . . . help? He'd asked if I had enough time, so maybe Reid asked him to not come for me right away, hoping we would come up with a plan.

"Yeah, I think we did," I said and he nodded, confirming my thoughts.

He hesitated and asked, "What am I supposed to do?"

"What you were told to do. Then let me handle the rest."

Kiato looked unsure, like once he took me, there was no going back. I wondered what Reid had said to him to change his mind. Maybe not *change* his mind, but at least something in the way of that.

The plan would have worked either way—this just gave us an advantage.

I stood and let him take my arm. Even though I was doing this on purpose, my stomach still had knots and my heart wouldn't stop hammering.

Everything depended on me.

Kiato drifted us to what looked like an old office in a warehouse. Buck was there, talking on the phone, and he visibly jumped when we appeared, looking pissed at Kiato. But when he saw I was with him, he smiled and hung up.

"*You*," he said. "Can't stay away, can you?"

No wonder Knox couldn't find Buck—he was the one behind everything. Were the other missing sliders here too?

I swallowed away my doubt and said, "It's a little hard when you have my whole family."

"And your boyfriend."

My breath hitched at that—just out of surprise from hearing the word.

Buck nodded, motioning me to come over to a set of windows overlooking the warehouse. Kiato gave me a warning look before letting go, probably just for Buck's sake. I stepped up to the window, and what I saw took my breath away.

Even though Buck was watching my face, I couldn't mask anything.

He was holding the drifters in what looked like stalls with cement walls, and he'd chained each of them to the floor. From this high up, I could see in most of them. I saw Logan and Jake, and the closest one held Reid.

He sat against the wall with his legs drawn up and his head resting on one arm, with the other on the floor, cuffed to a too-short chain. Reid flickered and jerked back against the wall, like waking himself up from a bad dream.

He had just tried to drift and couldn't.

186

Flicker. Snap. That's all it was.

"Are my parents—"

"They're fine. Whenever one of them gets too sick, I have Kiato make them drift somewhere."

"Why are you doing this?"

"I have people coming tomorrow morning—willing to pay for people like you."

"So you're doing this for money? That's it?"

Buck turned so suddenly that I thought he might hit me. But he stopped himself or maybe thought better of it.

He just brought his face closer to mine and growled, "I don't have to explain anything to you."

Buck grabbed my arm, a lot harder than Kiato had, and led me out the door and downstairs. I saw a lot more guards—probably other sliders—once we reached the bottom floor, and I hoped Knox had enough people to counter them.

We came around the corner and Reid lifted his head.

It was like time stopped without it really happening.

The look he gave me—it was like he would have done anything to keep me from being there. It was hard to imagine us anywhere else, though. Would we have been on the subway? Would Reid be making a new animal with folded paper while I watched, wishing he would kiss me instead of just looking at me like he wanted to?

It was always hard wondering about the what-ifs.

So instead of wondering, I decided to take hold of the moment and show Buck exactly who he was dealing with.

I gave Reid a smile, and then it began.

REID

IN MY DREAM, I WAS SOMEWHERE ELSE. AT FIRST, it was a forest and the bright sun was coming through the branches, luring me out onto a beach. It was the beach that I had met Jake on, but this time, the waves were small and nobody was surfing.

I thought about going home because I wasn't supposed to be there. My parents would have been angry if they found me gone, again, in the middle of the night when I was supposed to be asleep.

I had to get back home.

I drifted away, and then I was woken by the snap of the chain and my arm being pulled back. I let out a sharp breath and looked around, like I'd somehow forgotten where I was. My wrist stung now that the wound had reopened and, at some point while I was asleep, a headache formed at the back of my head.

I was dreaming, and I had tried to drift.

I settled back against the wall again. I had to make sure

not to fall asleep, but it was hard because there was nothing else to do.

The guards talked to themselves like we couldn't hear them—or maybe they didn't care—and the word was that the buyer was coming the next morning. I wasn't sure how I was supposed to sit here until then, doing nothing. Especially not sleeping.

The frequency Buck found seemed to only work when you were on the outside, trying to look in. Like a dead zone. It definitely screwed with my ability to know where we were, but I could still look out.

So once in a while, I would look for Sam, wherever she was in the world, and get glimpses of her. The thing about finding people, though, it was like seeing a snapshot. You saw whatever they were doing in the moment you thought of them and it was gone in a second. She was in the desert with Gavin once and then she was in a room full of people I didn't recognize.

I hoped whatever she was doing, it was working.

A door slammed—a sound I'd learned meant Buck was coming out of hiding. He had an office somewhere up top, and I could see the windows from where I was kept, but I rarely caught a glimpse of him.

But when he came around the corner, he wasn't alone.

Sam was with him.

Sam.

She wasn't supposed to be here. What happened? Where was Gavin? *She wasn't supposed to be here.* A heavy feeling of dread settled in my stomach. If Sam was here, it meant we weren't getting out of here at all.

Then Sam smiled at me, and I thought maybe I'd imagined it. Because why would she be smiling?

But I couldn't help loving it all the same. Sam's smile was contagious—I had noticed the first time I met her, sitting across from me on the subway. Who would have known such a mundane day could turn into something amazing?

There was suddenly a blur and then Sam was gone, leaving Buck looking like someone had slapped him in the face. Sam was now against the other wall of the warehouse, a good twenty feet between her and Buck, who was still confused about what happened.

She had slowed time—she hadn't drifted.

I stood, using the wall for support. Sam glanced to her left and her smile disappeared. Did she see her mom? Her brother? She didn't look long, bringing her focus back on Buck.

"Now hold on a minute," Buck said, his voice suddenly sounding like they were friends. "You know if you drift away, Kiato will just find you again."

Maybe he hadn't realized she didn't drift, or maybe he was ignoring the fact because he didn't know what to do with it. I glanced at Kiato, wondering if he would take control of the situation, but he was doing nothing but watching.

"You know one good thing about being a teenager?" Sam asked, facing him. "Everyone always underestimates you."

Then something *appeared* next to Sam. It was like the air cracked open beside her and a little rush of wind sounded off the walls. Like the sound of drifting.

Buck flinched back and I could do nothing but stare, shock keeping me in place more than the chain at my wrist.

Then someone stepped through the opening. It was Knox, and then Gavin appeared beside him, and then a dozen more people came through after them.

When the opening disappeared, Sam fell to one knee like she didn't have the strength to hold herself up. Her name got stuck in my throat and the chain snapped at my wrist. Her eyes found mine and she nodded once. After a moment, she stood.

Buck's guards were on high alert now that Knox and his

men were suddenly here without warning. Most of them had weapons but no guns, since they were mostly useless against sliders and drifters.

Knox narrowed his eyes at Buck, looking angrier by the second.

"It was you behind all of this?" Knox asked, shaking his head. "Stealing the list behind my back? I should have known. You just can't let the past die, can you?"

"Not when it doesn't deserve to be dead!" Buck flicked out a knife and Knox eyed it.

"I'm going to give you one chance," Knox told him. "Leave now before this gets worse."

Buck angled his body toward him and asked, "What happened to you? You hated drifters once, but now you're just a bleeding heart."

Knox paused and looked over at Gavin. When he looked at Buck again, he shrugged. "I think it's time things change."

"Your loss."

Buck surged forward and so did every slider in the room. The only weakness sliders had was they could only slow time for so long, so between the quick bursts of speed, there were fights dancing across the room in every direction.

I pressed myself against the wall and suddenly Sam was there in front of me. "Hi."

I smiled because I couldn't help myself. "Hi, are you okay?"

She looked worn out and tired, but at least she was standing again.

"Yeah, I'm fine." She looked down at the cuff around my wrist and said, "I need to go back up to the office to look for keys. I'll be right back."

Before I could respond, she drifted away.

Gavin slammed another slider against the wall next to me and then they were gone again in a dark blur.

I felt nothing but useless, unable to help, and hoped Buck had left the keys somewhere obvious for Sam to find. It was hard to keep track of who was fighting whom, and for a minute, I thought I saw Sabrina there. Then I saw her again, grabbing a slider from behind before drifting both of them away.

Sam came back, breathless, but with the key in hand. After a little bit of fumbling, she unlocked my cuff, and I grabbed her hand.

"Stay close, okay?"

She nodded and we took off down the line of stalls. We found Jake next, shocked to see us both there. His hair was halfway out of his usual neat bun and he wore only a T-shirt and jeans.

The relief I had at seeing him—not just hearing him through the walls—was unprecedented.

"Reid—" He didn't even finish his sentence before pulling me into a hug. My throat tightened and I couldn't say anything.

He finally pulled away and Sam unlocked him. I looked to see if our way was clear. The sliders still fought each other, but it definitely seemed like Knox's men were gaining some ground.

I caught sight of Gavin on the other side of the warehouse and, for a moment, it looked like he was done with his fight, standing over one of the guards. Then I saw movement behind him.

Buck, with a knife in his hand.

He didn't see him.

I took hold of Sam, saying in a rush, "Get the others out of here."

Jake said my name, but I was gone, drifting within shouting range, because drifting within arm's reach of a knife wasn't a good idea.

"*Gavin!*" My voice carried and Gavin looked up, hearing

192

me. Then he spun around, catching Buck's arm just in time. Another one of Buck's men saw them and started to close the distance.

I needed to get him out of here.

Something crashed into my back and I fell to the floor in a rush. The wind got knocked out of me and someone had their knee pressed into my back.

Gavin was trying to fight two sliders now, losing ground. He needed help.

I pushed up and to the left, dislodging the knee in my back, and got my feet under me. My attacker was already coming down on me again and nicked my jaw with his fist. I blocked the next blow, but I was distracted, trying to see where Gavin was.

I saw a flash of steel too close and I didn't turn in time.

Another hand closed around the knife, stopping it inches from my chest. Jake stood there, glaring at the slider.

"Reid, go," he said.

I backed away and searched for Gavin, knowing Jake could take care of himself. The place Gavin had been a moment ago was now empty, but there was an open door nearby. I started for it, dodging another fight on the way.

Through the door was another long hallway, but I saw light at the other end, like an open truck bay. I drifted to it and stepped outside. There was a body on the ground—the other slider. Hoping he was still alive, I went around him and down the steps, searching for Buck and Gavin.

I turned the corner and stopped short.

Gavin was slumped against the wall with a piece of rebar steel through his stomach. His hands were shaking and already covered in blood. His eyes caught mine and I'd never seen that look from him before—like something terrified him so much that he was speechless.

193

I dropped to my knees beside him. My hands could only hover over his wound because I didn't know what to do. Should I pull it out or leave it in?

Gavin took a shuddering breath and I locked eyes with him, putting a hand on his shoulder.

"You're going to be okay," I told him.

"Reid—"

"Have I ever lied to you?"

He had the audacity to look unsure about that and it made me laugh. I looked down at the rebar again and all the blood gushing out.

Gavin whispered, "I'm scared."

I met his eyes again and swallowed away whatever tried to come up.

"Well it's a good thing you're friends with a drifter," I said.

Jake came skidding around the corner, taking in the situation.

A shoe scuffed the asphalt behind me and, even though it took everything I had, I stood and turned away from Gavin. Buck glanced down at his work, like he wasn't sorry at all.

My blood ran red-hot and my fists clenched.

I glanced at Jake and said, "Take Gavin to a hospital."

And before Buck could say something smart, I drifted to him, grabbed his shoulder, and took him to a forest thousands of miles away in Canada. Huge trees surrounded us, and the forest floor was full of old mossy logs. Thunder growled in the distance.

"What are you going to do?" Buck asked, looking unimpressed. "Leave me here?"

"That would be too easy," I said.

I took off my jacket and set it at my feet. "You hate when I win those fights? Well, show me why I shouldn't."

My heart pounded as I challenged him like this. It was

probably the stupidest thing to do, but I couldn't let him think he won. He had hurt Gavin and deserved to pay for it. He deserved to pay for everything he'd done, and for what? Revenge? Bitterness? Money?

Buck smiled and then he was a blur. I drifted to the left, catching him off guard, and threw the first punch. I missed, or he was too fast. He was suddenly on my right, grabbing and twisting my arm.

I drifted us next to a tree and used his body weight to slam him into the trunk and then elbowed him as I spun away.

"All right, Reid." He spat out blood. "Let's see what you've really got."

He came at me again, and whenever I drifted, he was there waiting for me. I dodged blows and tried to hit him when there was nothing but air.

There was a reason drifters didn't go up against sliders in close combat: sliders always had the advantage. Buck was wearing me down and he knew it, but I also knew his slides were becoming shorter. He was losing strength too.

The next time he came at me, I drifted like I did in the fights. Instead of going far away like he was expecting, I drifted only a few inches to the left.

Buck's eyes widened in surprise, and I knocked him backward and he hit the ground. He finally stopped and just lay there, looking up at me. We were both breathing heavily.

"Are you going to finish me off, Reid?" he asked. "We both know you want to."

I shook my head and stepped back, even though the thought had crossed my mind. Did that make me a bad person, just thinking about it? Just to consider it? Dad's face flashed across my thoughts, smiling at me from across the dinner table.

I'm not sure what he would do in my situation, but I knew

stepping away from this fight was the right thing to do. I shouldn't have started it in the first place.

I didn't see Buck moving until it was too late.

A knife flashed in his hand, and I drifted without thinking.

SAM

NEW JERSEY, UNITED STATES

WHILE LOGAN HELPED ME FREE THE REST OF THE drifters, I caught a glimpse of Reid disappearing through the door at a run. It was hard not to be distracted by where he was going or what he was doing, but I needed to free everyone else.

Logan didn't even have shoes on, like Kiato really *had* found him while he was taking a nap, but he still had a grin on his face when I came for him.

"Sam, that was *amazing*! How did you do that?"

"If my assumptions are correct, you can probably do it too." But before he could get too excited, I said, "But now is not the time."

So we went down the line and found Mom and Dad, both of them hugging us too much and trying to ask too many questions I didn't have time for. After them, there were a few others I didn't have names for. One woman drifted away as soon as I unlocked her, and then we were done.

By the time everyone was free, Knox and his friends had taken control of the warehouse.

But then there was word that Gavin was hurt and Jake had

taken him to the closest hospital. Nobody knew how hurt, but Jake had found a slider just before taking Gavin away, so his family would know.

Knox was already on the phone, trying to find out where they were, and Dad was there with a hand on his shoulder.

But nobody seemed to remember that Buck was still missing, along with Reid. I quickly tried to find him, and I glimpsed him in a Canadian forest, blood dripping down his temple.

"I need to go," I said and Dad looked over at me. "Reid is with Buck right now and he needs help."

"Alex—" Knox said, the phone still to his ear. He had heard what I said, and he knew Buck was the one who wounded Gavin.

Dad turned to him and said, "I've got this. You go find Gavin."

A look passed between them; they didn't even need words. Knox finally nodded, silently thanking him. Dad came over to me, and Mom looked unsure about our going.

"You can follow us there," Dad offered.

"I will if you don't come back after a few minutes." She gave him a warning look.

Dad held out his hand and I took it, drifting us away immediately.

SAM

BRITISH COLUMBIA, CANADA

WE DRIFTED TO THE FOREST JUST IN TIME TO SEE Reid drifting away. Buck stood there alone, holding a knife in his hand. The forest we drifted into was full of huge trees with green moss inching up their trunks and spreading over the grassy floor. Wind rocked the high branches—a promise of a coming storm.

Why had Reid brought them here? Did he just want to get Buck away from Gavin, or did he bring him here hoping for a fight?

Dad approached Buck slowly, and I followed behind.

"It's over, Buck," Dad called out. "You don't have to make this any harder."

"Back in the day, you would have approved of what I was doing."

"I was a different person back then," Dad agreed. "But that's definitely a stretch, even for you."

Buck shrugged. "Apparently not. So what's it going to be? Will you take me back to Knox? Have him *deal* with me?"

"Maybe we'll leave you in your warehouse for your buyer to find," Dad said.

Buck laughed, nodding. "That's a good one, even for you."

"Just trying to play on your level." Dad got serious again and said, "I didn't think you'd ever do something like this. I know you've always been angry about your father, but this was too far."

"You don't know what it's like to have an anger inside you so great that it feels like it's consuming you. After all these years, it felt like I was burning, and then I found I could do something about it—that I could channel it and force them to feel what I felt. To make them pay."

Buck stuck the knife in a nearby log, and once I got a closer look at it, my breath caught in my throat.

It was covered in blood. *Reid.*

Buck noticed my reaction and said, "Guess he wasn't fast enough." He shrugged.

Dad glanced at me, eyebrows pulled together, and asked Buck, "What did you do?"

"Nothing he wasn't asking for."

Dad saw the look on my face and said, "Sam, go. Your mom will be here soon."

"Might already be too late," Buck said.

I didn't want to leave him with Buck, but I also needed to find Reid. Dad nodded at me again, and I left.

SAM

ALASKA, UNITED STATES

THE FIRST THING I SAW WAS A SPLASH OF RED against the snow. It was just a dusting over the grass, probably one of the first snowfalls of the year. It was still white enough to see the blood, as clear as day. A trail of it followed a pair of footprints and I pushed past a few evergreens and stopped short.

Reid stood with his back to me, just wearing his black T-shirt, which outlined his figure against the snow-covered trees. He stood leaning a little to the right, so his hips weren't perfectly aligned, like he'd been standing there all day, tired and worn out.

I started toward him, but he didn't react, so I wasn't sure if he'd heard me. I stopped at his side. He didn't glance my way, just kept staring forward.

"Reid?"

Gaining enough courage, I forced my eyes down to find his wound, just beneath his ribs. His right hand covered it, doing nothing to hold in the blood. It ran over his fingers and dripped onto the ground. His body was probably still in shock from what happened, and he didn't seem to be in any pain yet.

When I looked back to his face, his eyes still stared ahead. I finally followed his gaze.

At first, I saw nothing but forest, but the longer I stared, the more something took shape among the branches. It was a house, hidden under the canopy of trees. It looked like nobody had touched it in years.

"This is where I grew up," Reid said. His fingers twitched over his wound and he flinched. "And this is where my parents died."

Then I understood why he came here, quickly drifting away from Buck and his knife.

It was his drift point, where he drifted when he didn't have time to think of anywhere else.

My eyes traveled over the house again. I was unable to imagine what he went through every time he came here. No wonder he didn't like talking about his past—there was nothing but heartbreak.

"I'm sorry I lied to you." Finally, he tore his gaze from the cabin and looked at me. "I don't know why I didn't tell you, but I should have. It's such a stupid thing to lie about. Maybe I was afraid of losing you."

"Why would you lose me?"

He gave me a very sad kind of smile. "Because I seem to lose everyone who gets close to me. You know I'm not perfect, far from it, and my past always haunts me no matter what I do." He shrugged one shoulder. "I wasn't there when they died, and I still don't know who was responsible. And for some reason, this seems to be the place I always come back to." Reid looked at the house again, breathing a little heavier. "It's my drift point, even when I don't want it to be."

His free hand lay limp by his side and I took it, brushing my fingers over his knuckles.

Reid closed his eyes and his fingers tightened around mine.

"You haven't lost me yet," I said, "and you're not going to. You may have a different past than I do, but that doesn't change who you are now. It doesn't change that I care about you."

He opened his eyes, but they were still downcast, lashes dark against his skin. "You've meant more to me in this past week than anybody has in a long time." He caught my eye. "I just keep thinking it's too good to be true. Or I'll somehow ruin it."

"Then it's a good thing you can always find me," I joked.

A half of a smile appeared. "I'm serious, Sam."

I allowed my smile to fade away. "I'm not going anywhere, and if I ever do, know that it isn't by choice. Nothing about your past is going to make me leave."

"You don't get it," he whispered, looking at the house again. "I always woke up in the middle of the night, and instead of going back to sleep, I would drift somewhere. My parents always tried to make me stop, but I was just a kid, you know? But that night when I came back—it was too late."

"Why do you think it's a bad thing?" I asked. "You might've been killed with them."

"But what if I could have helped them?" he asked, desperate. "That's what I hate most. I keep thinking I could have saved them. I could have helped somehow."

"You were just a kid . . . you can't blame yourself."

Reid winced as a shiver ran through his body. He closed his eyes, trying to ignore the pain and the fact he was still bleeding. He needed to get to a hospital.

"I haven't gone in there since it happened," he said, nodding toward the cabin. "When I come here, I usually leave straight away, so I don't have to remember. I keep thinking I'll have enough courage to walk through that door, to face what I left behind. But I never do."

203

"Maybe someday you will."

"Maybe."

When Reid turned toward me, I knew it was another one of those moments he was thinking about kissing me, and I wanted him to. But now was probably the worst timing for it.

"We should go," I told him. "You need a doctor."

Reid glanced down to his hand, moving it slightly away from the wound. He studied it. He nodded, still looking down.

I tightened my hand around his and drifted to a hospital in San Diego, appearing in the parking lot across the street. I still remembered this place from years ago, when I sprained my wrist on vacation, so maybe that's why it was the first one I thought of.

The streets were quiet with just a few cars, and the people walking by didn't seem to notice anything was wrong with us. I took a step toward the hospital, but Reid held me back.

"You're not coming with me," he said.

He looked ready to fall over, clenching his jaw in pain.

"Reid—" I opened and closed my mouth twice before I knew what I wanted to say. "I just found you—I don't want to leave you already."

"I know, but you have to. If you come with me, they'll ask you questions that you can't answer. It's better if they know nothing about me, or you."

I had to admit, his explanation made sense. Even though I hated it.

"What will you tell them?"

"I'm not going to tell them anything. I'm going to get stitched up and leave the first moment I get. If I have to, I'll tell them I don't remember anything, or give them a fake name." Reid's eyes found mine. "Trust me. I've had experience with this before."

I smiled but couldn't hold it. "I guess I'm not surprised, but how will I know you're going to be okay?"

"I'll be fine. Once I get out, I promise I'll find you again."
I looked away, forcing the lump in my throat to stay where it
was. "Sam, look . . ." He stepped closer, his breathing hitching
in his throat. "I don't want you to look for me either, not even
a glimpse."

I hated that he had asked that, but I had to respect his
privacy.

"I won't," I promised.

His hand came up to my face, his touch setting my skin on
fire. "But when I do see you, I promise that we'll finally have
that kiss." A dimple appeared with his half smile.

"Don't make me wait too long, or I really will come to find
you," I warned.

He gave a low laugh.

Reid took a step back toward the hospital with his hand
covering the wound. He was pale again, almost on the verge
of collapsing, and I was afraid he would, but he finally turned
and walked across the street. I could tell that every step was
an effort.

The feeling I had while I watched him walk away, not
knowing when I would see him next, was nearly unbearable.

Someone outside the hospital's revolving door shouted
when they saw Reid. A couple of EMTs ran toward him. He
took a bad step and staggered to the ground, no longer able to
hold himself up.

I couldn't watch any longer. My last image of him wasn't
a pleasant one. His hand, limp and bloodied, lying motion-
less next to him as hospital staff surrounded him. The hardest
thing to do was drift away.

REID

CALIFORNIA, UNITED STATES

I REMEMBERED FALLING DOWN OUTSIDE THE hospital doors. I remembered somebody shouting to get help. I vaguely remembered being brought into the building.

It was all a blur.

Until the pain became so bad that unconsciousness wouldn't even take over. Bright lights flashed in my eyes, upside-down heads appeared over me, and people talked without pause. A heavy pressure on my stomach made it hard to breathe.

And I lay there, watching the world spin around me as they tried to patch me up. I could feel every time someone touched the wound and every moment I took a breath.

When the pain got bad, I clenched my fists and closed my eyes, imagining myself away from here but forcing myself to stay. I had to stay, and I wondered what they would think if I disappeared before their eyes. The thought made everything a little more bearable, taking my mind off the pain.

I felt a sharp prick in my side, and then a steady beeping in my ears quickened, too fast. I wanted to sleep. I wanted to wake up and have the nightmare be over.

My wish came true a moment later when the medicine hit my veins. I closed my eyes, waiting for nothingness to overtake me.

It was about time.

My eyelids were heavy when I first tried to open them. Every muscle in my body felt weighted down, whispering for me to go back to sleep. When I finally blinked awake, I was alone. I was always alone, so I should have expected it, but for some reason, it surprised me. The last time I was awake, there were so many people around, I just figured there still would be.

How long ago was that?

A vacant chair sat next to my bed, and for a very brief instant, I wished Jake were there.

The door to my room stood open, showing the half-lit hallway. I had no way of telling what time it was, but it had to be sometime in the night because the hospital was quiet and no natural light came from the window.

An IV was connected to my arm, and beeping came from the machine next to me. I couldn't move anything but my head, my body feeling so heavy and tired, but I could see one of my wrists wrapped in white cloth. When I tried to move my fingers, they responded, twitching and feeling the blanket under them.

I had never felt so tired before, so drained of life.

I assumed this was from whatever medicine they had pumped into me.

I never minded being alone—it was who I was, and it was the only thing that I knew. But I was hurting and tired, and being in a hospital, so far away from the only home I had, made me yearn for some company.

I wondered how long I would have to stay there, and even debated if I would be fine if I left right then. But I wasn't sure how much damage had been done. I decided to wait, at least until the doctor could fill me on what I didn't know.

Then I would leave.

A soft breeze rushed into the room, warning me.

My heart quickened until I saw Jake at the foot of my bed. His hair looked more disheveled than usual, and for once he wasn't smiling or smirking. He looked over me once, like he was making sure I was alive, before he walked to the door, shutting it quietly so the nurses down the hall wouldn't hear.

In his arms, he held the jacket I had left in the forest with Buck. He also brought an extra pair of clothes, which meant he had gone to my apartment at some point. He draped them over the chair and sat down, sighing.

He didn't put his legs up on the bed—again, surprising. He had something on his mind.

"Look—" he started, having a hard time meeting my eyes. "I'm sorry for not being there for you more than I was."

"You have been," I replied, hesitant.

"Not as much as I should have."

As much as I would have liked to admit that I didn't care, I really did. Whenever Jake came around, he stayed about five minutes unless I spent the night at his place—which wasn't that often.

I never had the nerve to bring it up.

I never wanted to admit I needed help.

I looked away and lay back on my pillow. "Why are we talking about this right now?"

"Because seeing Kiato bring you in that night when I couldn't help you, I felt like I somehow could have prevented it. Like maybe if I was around more, you wouldn't get into so many fights, and Buck wouldn't have taken so much notice of you and then he wouldn't have sent Kiato after—"

"*Stop*," I said. "None of this is your fault, okay? I—"

I could feel my heart beating a little faster, his eyes staring into mine, and I wanted to drift so badly right then, just to get away from his steady gaze. He waited, knowing I wasn't finished.

"It's just—" I closed my mouth, battling myself to say what I wanted. "There was this one time I drifted to somewhere in Iowa. It was literally in the middle of nowhere, just corn for miles and empty roads. I was at this gas station, and someone else was there waiting outside on the curb. Another kid, around my age. He looked so alone and I almost said something to him, but then an old truck pulled up and a man got out, asking him if he was okay and hugged him. You could *hear* the worry in his voice."

I paused and glanced at Jake. "And I couldn't help but think—I don't have anyone like that. Someone to call and they'll come, no questions asked."

"But you do," Jake said, leaning forward.

"I know," I said, nodding. I could feel the first tears run down my cheeks and I said again, "I know."

"No, look at me." Jake put a hand on the back of my neck, coming closer to make sure I saw him. "Remember how we first met? You were so young and happy, and I knew after that day, my life wouldn't be the same without you."

I could only nod.

Jake said, "I will *always* be there for you. Because that's what brothers do. You hear me?"

"Okay," I replied. Because that's all I could say.

Jake sniffed once and pulled back. "Okay then."

I found the strength to swipe at my cheeks. "Thank you for coming." I said it so softly, I wasn't sure if he had heard me.

But Jake nodded. "Of course."

"What happened with everyone? Is Gavin okay?"

"Gavin will be in the hospital for a while, but yeah, he'll be fine. I stayed to make sure, and then I got hold of Knox to let him know where we were. I heard after you and Buck left, things settled down pretty fast. Thankfully nobody was killed."

Jake glanced at me, wanting to say something else.

"What?" I asked.

"Why did you take Buck? Where did you go?"

I shrugged and admitted, "I'm not really sure. I just wanted to *fight* him, you know? After everything he did, I just wanted . . . I don't know. It was dumb, okay?"

"Not dumb," Jake said. "Just human."

"Where is he now?" I asked.

"Knox has him—so not our problem anymore."

"And the buyers?"

"Well, they'll show up to an empty warehouse that was bleached top to bottom because we didn't want to leave behind any samplings. Buck was their only contact."

"You think we'll have trouble with them in the future?"

"The possibility of being exposed has always been there, you know that."

I did know it and always tried to ignore it, just trying to live life without worrying every minute of every day. But maybe that wasn't the right mindset to have. Maybe I needed to be more careful about drifting in front of people. We never knew who could be watching.

"We're lucky we had Sam," I finally said. "Without her . . ."

Jake nodded. "What she did was . . . I don't even have words for it. I've never seen anything like it."

"Me either."

Jake sat back, putting his feet up on the bed. It made me happy—it meant he wasn't in a rush to leave. "I'm curious to know if Logan can too. Things have definitely changed." He eyed me. "Including you."

"What's that supposed to mean?"

"You're different now that you have Sam. In a good way."

The monitor that observed the rhythm of my heart spiked when Jake mentioned her. He grinned, noticing the different speed. It was the way he'd said it: *Now that you have Sam.* I felt it was proof we were together, and that was something to make my stomach fly.

"You see what I mean? I've never seen you smile so much. And trust me, you could use more of it." He grinned widely. "You're growing up, little brother."

This kind of affection he was showing me was new, but it settled in my heart as if it had always belonged there. It was true that Jake was always like an older brother to me, but I had never embraced it like I should have.

It felt good to have someone watching out for me, because most of the time, it felt like I was alone. I knew now that wasn't true.

"Thanks, Jake." There were no joking tone in my voice, or a hint of sarcasm. I really meant it.

He nodded once. "Just remember, you know where I live, and there will always be an open room for you." He stood but paused near my bed. "I don't want you to leave here until you're ready, because I know if it was up to you, you would be gone by morning." I opened my mouth to protest, but he cut me off. "No, you're staying. I'm going to go throw some cash at them for their silence. As for the questions, just tell them that you don't remember anything."

I wanted to argue, but there was honestly nothing to argue about. Sam was the only reason for me to leave, but I knew she wasn't going anywhere. I already missed her, but I'd also never been this hurt before.

"Fine, I'll stay, but only until I'm well enough to leave."

"That's all I'm asking." He nodded once. "I'll see you later."

Once Jake left, the tiredness seeped back into my muscles and bones. I felt like I could sleep the night away and then the whole day after. The strong desire to see Sam lingered within my heart and chest, but it wasn't time. I had to heal before I could see her because I knew once I did, I would never want to leave her side.

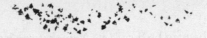

I slept through the morning and most of the afternoon, vaguely remembering nurses coming in to check on me through my sleeping haze. When I woke in the late afternoon, they gave me food and I ate it all within minutes. Doctors and nurses kept coming in after hearing that I was finally awake, and they all wanted to know what happened.

Just as Jake told me to do, I told them I didn't remember.

There was one nurse in particular that keep muttering under her breath in Spanish as she checked my wound. She was probably in her early thirties with long hair drawn back into a messy bun.

I winced when she touched my wound too hard, and she finally acknowledged I was there. Until then, she had been off in her own world, or maybe one that made her concentrate on her job. Either way, she hadn't yet spoken to me.

"I know you remember what happened," she said. Although she mainly spoke Spanish, she didn't have any sort of accent. She replaced the bandage over the stitches and pulled my shirt back down. "I'm Katrina."

I clenched my jaw as she studied me. Instead of playing dumb, I asked, "How can you tell?"

"You don't have a head wound bad enough. Second of all, your *brother* has an accent and you don't."

"We didn't grow up together. Different dads in different countries." It was a good lie. Even *I* was impressed with myself.

"Then how do you explain the lacerations around your wrist? You'll be very lucky if they don't scar."

I glanced down at my wrist wrapped in a white bandage and didn't meet her eyes again. "I guess when I hit my head, it made me forget," I said. The gash on my head only needed a couple stitches, and she was right—it wasn't even that bad of a head wound, but I kept up with the lie anyway.

"Reid."

I looked up. It was weird hearing my name come out of her mouth. None of the other nurses had addressed me by name. They probably thought it was fake—the last name in my chart was, but not my first. "If this is something that's going on at home, you need to tell someone."

"No, it's nothing like that," I said and held her gaze.

She removed the IV from my arm and eyed me. "If you say so."

I changed the subject. "No more drugs?"

"No, so be prepared for a rough night." She turned to leave but paused, her eyes sweeping over me once. She gestured her hand over me. "I'm going to bring you more food before the cafeteria closes. You're too skinny."

That night I became restless. I wasn't made for staying in a bed for days on end. It felt good to be free of the tubes finally, and I drifted to the roof and back a few times, waiting for my body to become tired enough to sleep. I didn't think I could lie around for another day, and I fell asleep around two o'clock with the thought that I would leave in the morning.

But when morning came, I was awakened by Katrina entering my room. She looked flustered and not at all happy. I sat up, attempting to hold my hand over the ache in my side. "What is it?"

She said something in Spanish. It sounded like a curse word. Then she stopped and stared at me. Her eyes shifted to the door, thinking hard about something. "Some people from child services are downstairs. They got word of you. And your *brother*, who paid the bill, didn't give us any real contact information."

I needed to leave. It didn't matter if I was ready or not, it was time. My heart pounded hard, but I reminded myself that they couldn't keep me here even if they wanted to.

"When are they coming?"

"Soon." She must have seen it in my eyes, because she came closer and put a hand on my arm. "Just breathe for a moment, okay?"

I nodded because she was right. I was already starting to freak out. I kept thinking about the night Mom and Dad died, when I waited in that office until I couldn't take it anymore.I couldn't do that again.

I needed to *leave*.

"Reid, look at me." I looked. "Whatever is going on with you, you can tell me."

"I can't be put into the system," I said, hurriedly. "I won't."

"What happened? Did you have a bad experience? If you did, you need to report it."

I was already shaking my head. "No, no, it's not that. It's just—" I paused, wondering if I could trust her. "I'm almost eighteen, so there's no point."

"No point in what?"

"No point in starting."

I saw the moment she realized what I meant. She stood and came around to sit in the empty chair next to the bed.

"You need to tell me the truth when I ask these next questions, okay? Because I cannot, in my good conscience, let you leave until I know you'll be taken care of. Has this happened before?" She gestured to my wrist and my stomach.

"No."

"How long have you been living on your own?"

There was a roar in my ears and my heart pounded. "A few years," I said, almost a whisper.

Katrina nodded. "You know, I was in the foster system when I was younger."

The roaring lessoned a little. "You were?"

"Yes. I was scared at first—you know, all those horror stories in movies and books about bad foster parents. And yes, there are real stories too. But you know what? Most of the homes aren't like that. The people are doing it because they *want* to help kids in situations like yours."

"I know."

She cocked her head, smiling. "Do you?"

I tried not to smile and said, "Maybe they should have someone like you working for them."

Her smile slowly vanished. "When I meet kids like you, I wish I was."

"You don't have to worry about me, I promise. My birthday is coming up. There's no point now."

She nodded and asked her final question. "Are you living somewhere safe?"

I hesitated and another voice spoke in my place. "He's living with me. I'll even give you the address if you want to check it out yourself," Jake said, standing in the doorway.

Katrina looked back at me and I nodded.

Jake said, "We might not be blood, but we're still brothers."

"Then I suggest you both leave before they come looking." She put a hand on my arm and said, "You take care of yourself, okay?"

I nodded, and once she left, Jake asked, "You ready to go?"

"Yeah."

It took me a little while to get dressed. Jake offered to help, but I needed to do it on my own, to prove to myself I was still strong and able. After a few minutes, I was ready to go—jeans, T-shirt, jacket, bag over shoulder, and hair its usual unkempt way.

Then I was gone. This time not alone.

SAM

NEW YORK, UNITED STATES

AFTER LEAVING REID AT THE HOSPITAL, THE NEXT twenty-four hours was a blur. Mostly because I needed to sleep, and I did, from early that evening until late the next morning. I was supposed to go to school, but Mom called them, first apologizing for my missed days and then letting them know I wouldn't be there until tomorrow.

I got a new phone and texted Nella right away, letting her know I was safe and everything was okay, and that I would see her at school—which felt weird even thinking about. I had traveled to countless countries in just a couple days and now I had to go back to school?

I wasn't sure how I could manage it.

But for the first time in a long time, my whole family was under the same roof, which made being normal a little more bearable. Logan was stalling going back to school, and even though he should have gone back by now, I was happy he hadn't yet.

When I went downstairs for breakfast, he was sitting at the table eating cereal. He looked like he'd just rolled out of bed, and I wished he were there, looking like that, every morning.

I sat down next to him and poured myself a bowl.

Even though we were out of immediate danger, it was hard going back to "normal" life. Especially since normal life before now never consisted of us talking about how we had these abilities. It had always been a secret to me, and I was still trying not to be bitter about it.

The day before, Mom wouldn't leave my room until I halfway forgave her.

She kept saying, "It was for your own safety, I promise." And "I wish I could have been there for you."

I knew she would have been if Buck hadn't taken them both, so part of it wasn't her fault.

It was just a lot all at once.

And the biggest thing? My whole family kept looking at me like I had two heads because they had all seen what happened in that warehouse, and nobody knew what to do about it, or how to talk about it.

I found myself wishing I could talk to Reid, which didn't feel right when my family was already there.

Mom came into the kitchen then, glancing at us both before pouring herself a cup of coffee. Dad came in next, and I suddenly knew what was about to happen.

We were going to have a *talk*.

Logan and I shared a quick look as our parents sat down at the table. Would I have gotten into trouble if I just drifted away? Probably. I still wanted to do it. Logan looked like he wanted to disappear too.

"We need to talk about what happened," Mom announced.

Logan peeked over at me, shifting uncomfortably in his seat.

"Look," I said, wanting to get it over with. "You guys didn't tell me about *anything* and that's okay. I get it, I really do. But I don't want secrets between us anymore."

Dad said, "We don't want that either. That's why we're here."

"So just to make it clear, you guys had no idea that Logan or I could inherit both your abilities?"

Mom and Dad glanced at each other, and Dad finally said, "Logan never showed any signs, but we always thought there might be a possibility."

Logan spoke up next, leaning forward a bit. "But you also never *told* me that. Maybe if you asked me to try, we would have known for sure."

"There's not a guidebook for this stuff, okay?" Dad said, looking a bit frustrated at the situation. "We were doing what we thought best, and we're sorry if we messed up somewhere along the way."

After a moment of silence, I said, "It doesn't matter, dwelling on the past. That's what Buck did and look what happened."

Dad nodded and Mom said, "You're right."

"So when Sam uses both abilities, she somehow messes with space and time and creates some sort of rift?" Logan paused there, waiting for us to react.

I couldn't help myself. I had to laugh, just from the way he said it. "Yeah, but I wouldn't recommend it. I had a nasty headache for a whole day afterward."

"Laugh all you want," he told me. "But it's pretty cool. Plus . . . you sort of saved everyone."

"You were amazing," Mom agreed, looking at me in a way she hadn't before. Everyone was staring at me and I hated it. But the tension between us was suddenly gone and I felt at home again.

"Hopefully, that's the last time it needs to happen."

Logan muttered, "Under those circumstances." I gave him a look and he said, "What? It's really cool, and who knows when it'll come in handy."

After that, there wasn't much serious talk. Logan kept coming up with elaborate things to do with the "rift," and what he would do with his once he figured it out. He always knew how to make me laugh.

Dad finally got up, saying he was meeting Knox for lunch, and I wondered for the first time if this was the start of peace between drifters and sliders. Looking around at my family, though, I realized it had started way before now.

REID

TEXAS, UNITED STATES

AFTER WE LEFT THE HOSPITAL, JAKE TOOK ME OUT to eat at a diner in Texas. The place was packed, but we were able to find a free booth in the corner. The employees knew him by name, and he didn't even have to tell them what he wanted to eat. They already knew.

It felt good to be back in the world again. Where I could just eat pancakes and make jokes with Jake, even though my side hurt every time I laughed. It felt good to just *be*.

After we finished eating, Jake took me back to his new apartment. I was expecting something similar to the last one—a nice city view with glass walls, expensive furniture, and a luxury bathroom.

Instead, he brought me to a small apartment in Brooklyn with brick walls and no high tower view. It was sparsely furnished, but with *normal* furniture. Like something you would buy secondhand, but I couldn't imagine Jake buying a couch that someone else had owned.

"This—is your new place?" I asked, confused.

"Well, yeah, it's all I can afford, what with starting a new job."

I rounded on him. "*You* got a job?"

"Christ, don't act so surprised. I'm not as dense as I pretend to be, you know. I've been hearing what you say and you're right—even though we have these abilities, it doesn't mean we should take advantage of them. I figured it was time to put my degree to good use. Which means no more stealing." Then he pointedly looked at me and added, "And no more fighting."

"If you don't steal, I won't fight," I promised.

"And now that I have a job, you have to go back to school." He saw my face and put a hand up, stopping me. "That's the rule with you living here. You're going to get your diploma or GED or *whatever*, I don't care. No more cutting corners. If you've been going to enough of those college classes, you'll be able to jump right into your senior year."

School. I hadn't thought about school in so long. Just the normalization of school scared me. Having a normal *life* scared me.

I wasn't sure if I knew how.

Jake put a hand on my shoulder and said, "You aren't alone, okay? You wanna see your room?"

That put a small smile on my lips. "You aren't going to put me on the couch?"

"If I did, I don't think you'd stay."

"I still would."

I looked at him and he looked at me. For the second time, he was out of words.

Jake nodded to the right. "Come on, I'll show you."

He pushed a sliding door to reveal a bedroom with windows facing the street and a new bed in the middle, freshly made with new sheets and a new comforter. The dresser was empty, ready to be filled with the few possessions I had, and the walls were empty. Like a fresh slate.

"I guess this beats where I've been staying," I admitted.

Jake gave my shoulder a squeeze and said, "Welcome home."

After I moved half my stuff into the room, I left to see Gavin. He would have been in the hospital still, but his family had enough money to bring him home and hire a nurse to be there day and night.

I thought about knocking on the front door, announcing my presence, but there was a chance his family wouldn't let me see him.

So in my usual fashion, I drifted right into his room.

Gavin happened to be drinking a glass of water when I appeared, and he choked on some of it.

He coughed out, "Please, by all means, just come on in and make yourself at home."

His room was neat, looking as if someone had cleaned it from top to bottom before he came home. It was on the second floor, and his huge floor-to-ceiling windows had a view of the pool. Today the curtains were halfway closed and the TV on the dresser was playing a show on mute.

"Glad you're feeling well enough for sarcasm." I took the empty chair next to his bed and grinned at him. "You hungry?"

Gavin rolled his eyes. "Sorry, the bank is closed today." He lay back on his pillows and asked, "Is that all you came here for?"

I knew what I needed to say—I just didn't know how to start. Gavin was my best friend, so why was it so hard to talk about this?

Seeing my hesitation, Gavin asked, "What's wrong?"

"I came to say I'm sorry," I said in a rush.

"For what?"

Shouldn't he have already known? Shouldn't he have been angry at me? This would have been easier if he had told me to leave, or maybe if he had even thrown something at me. At least then I wouldn't have to explain.

"I left you, Gavin. I left you when you needed me the most.

I—" I opened and closed my mouth, finally shaking my head. "And I'll always regret it."

"Reid." Gavin stopped there, like he didn't know what to say. "What I saw . . . was you taking away the threat. Buck. If you hadn't taken him away, who knows what he could have done. He probably would have finished me off just to piss off my dad. You didn't leave me, Reid." He took a breath. "You saved me."

I searched Gavin's eyes, trying to understand what he had just said. Whatever way I thought about it, it wasn't what I knew to be true.

"I don't see it that way," I whispered.

"You came to find me when nobody else did," he said. "And then when you left, you left me with one of the only people you trust. If Jake hadn't been there, would you have done it?"

"Of course not."

"Then please, stop beating yourself up about things that don't matter. I was hurt, and you were making sure I would be safe."

I couldn't hold his gaze any longer and glanced at the TV for a distraction. It was on a home improvement show, and I wondered if it was on mute because he just wanted something to sleep to or if he actually enjoyed watching it.

I wish I already knew the answer and didn't have to guess.

Did it make me a bad friend for not knowing something so simple?

"Do you like this show?" he asked.

"I've never seen it."

Gavin found the remote and turned the sound back on. "You'll love it after one episode," he promised.

I guess I had my answer.

That's what I loved most about Gavin—he always made me feel like I was enough.

SAM

NEW YORK, UNITED STATES

I'D GONE BACK AND FORTH TO SCHOOL THE NEXT day with nobody sitting next to me and no sign of the boy who had once smiled at me and made me a paper elephant. The temptation to take a glimpse of him was strong, especially knowing I could at any moment. But I kept my promise, knowing he'd come when he was ready.

Mom and Dad kept asking me questions about Reid, and I told them as much as I could. As much as I knew about him, anyway.

When I got home from school, I avoided both of them and went up to my room. Logan was already there, lounging across my bed.

"Hey, slacker, you ready to go back to school?" I asked, dropping my bag on the floor.

School sucked. I couldn't concentrate in any of my classes and I didn't want to be there at all. Nella kept looking at me weird too, like I was going to disappear at any given moment. But all things considered, she was taking it well.

Mom yelled from downstairs, "Family dinner tonight! Logan is leaving tomorrow!"

I raised an eyebrow at him. "Finally, huh?"

"Can't miss any more classes."

"Want to take an early field trip?" I asked.

It took him a moment to catch on and he sat up. "Where do you have in mind?"

"Before we do anything that you might be thinking, I need to make a stop first."

Logan swung his legs off the bed. "Let me find my shoes," he said, looking a little too eager to get out of the house.

When he was ready to go, I took him to L.A., drifting in front of the door of a house that was way too big. The driveway was gated and the hedges were high enough to block out everything around.

Logan raised an eyebrow as I pressed the doorbell.

A guy answered the door wearing nothing but sweatpants. His hair said he had woken up not too long ago.

"Do I know you?"

"Is Kiato here?"

Logan looked over sharply, somehow holding his tongue. I pretended not to notice, and the guy finally nodded and let us in.

"Kiato! Someone's here to see you!"

Noise came from the kitchen and Kiato stepped into the hall. His shoulders tensed when he saw us.

"What are you doing here?" he asked.

"I just want to talk."

He hesitated, finally nodding for us to come in. The guy who opened the door followed us to the living room, where the remnants of a late breakfast sat on the coffee table.

"You good?" the guy asked Kiato.

"Yeah, it's fine."

"I'm gonna go take that shower then."

Logan waited until the guy was gone before asking, "Does he know about you?"

Kiato eyed where he left and shook his head. "Not yet. I'm trying to gain the courage."

Logan nodded. "I feel like there's always a sweet spot. Too soon, they go running. Too late and they won't trust you anymore."

I eyed Logan, wondering if he had firsthand experience. It's not something we had ever talked about, obviously.

"I feel like it's almost there," Kiato agreed. He finally looked at me and asked, "Why are you here?"

"I wanted to make sure you and your sister were okay. You disappeared pretty fast."

"Because everyone knows what I did," he said, anger underlining his tone. "I'm honestly surprised nobody has tried to come for me yet."

"Everyone knows what you did," I agreed. "But they also know you helped us in the end. Any one of us would have done the same if Buck had decided to target our family instead of yours."

Kiato sat back and looked out the window. "My sister is staying with my parents for a while. She was in college but that's put on hold now."

"Was she hurt?"

"Not physically."

Logan said, "I'm sorry."

Kiato glanced at him. "I'm sorry too."

"I can't speak for everyone, but nobody in our family has hard feelings," I told him. "We all saw what was happening."

"Without Reid, I'm not sure it would have gone the way it did." He shrugged. "He made me see there was another option."

Reid had a way of doing that—I was seeing that more and more.

There wasn't much more to say. Kiato showed us out, and once the door was closed, Logan clapped his hands and said, "Now let's go do something fun. We have about an hour before dinner—which means I can't take you to my favorite ramen place—but I can show you another cool place."

He took me to Universal Studios, giddy with himself because we didn't have to pay to get inside. The only thing he wanted to do was the *Transformers* 3-D ride, and I had to admit, it was a lot of fun even though the line was really long for it. I caught a glimpse of Hogwarts from a distance but we had to get back.

Logan told me, "Next time. You can finally get that wand."

Next time. Because this was never going away.

On Friday, days after leaving Reid at the hospital, I stood on the platform and waited for my train. The cold nipped at my neck and face, reminding me of the coming season. I had always loved winter. I loved wearing coats and hats, and especially boots. I loved the way the city looked after a fresh snow.

Now snow reminded me of Reid's family home and I wondered if it had the same effect on him.

I could have started drifting to school, but I couldn't give up the chance to see Reid. The train reminded me of him too much to stop riding it.

Over the normal subway sounds—people walking by and chatting with their friends, the constant hum from the subway tunnel—something very soft touched my ears, like a whisper.

I knew exactly what it was, and I closed my eyes, hoping more than anything it was him.

With a beating heart, I opened my eyes and turned. Reid stood on the platform, looking the same as the first day I saw him. His messenger bag across his chest, dark hair windswept as always, and his relaxed posture was every bit him. My heart wouldn't stop; I was worried it was a dream.

There was only one thing I wanted to do.

"You promised me something," I said.

Reid smiled, not fully, but enough for a hint of his dimple to appear. His dark eyes were bright, more alive than I'd ever seen.

When he took a step toward me, I could feel every vein pulsing fast and steady. Then he was there, he was next to me, inches away. I took in his scent of fresh air and wind. When he leaned in closer, his hand came up, his fingers slipping through my hair, past my ear.

"Your train just left without you," he whispered against my mouth.

I closed my eyes and smiled. "I know a way to catch it."

Then he kissed me, and his lips tasted like the wind.

ONE WEEK LATER

SOMETIMES I WANTED TO DISAPPEAR, AND SOME-
times I forgot I could, like old habits dying hard. I would day-
dream about being somewhere, wishing and hoping, and then
I would remember who I was.

Mrs. Stevens cleared her throat, and the whole class stared
at me, waiting for an answer that wouldn't come. The white-
board was wiped clean, giving away no hints. For a moment, I
even forgot what class I was in.

History. But what were we learning about?

"I take it you don't have an answer then?" Mrs. Stevens asked.

I shook my head and someone let out a breath of a laugh.

Mrs. Stevens looked over sharply, "Clara, don't think
you can hide that smile behind your book. Would you like
to answer for Sam? It seems her mind is on more important
things than this class."

If only she knew.

Even after returning to school, my mind was on everything
except schoolwork. It was hard to act normal when I knew I
wasn't.

I had no idea how Logan did it, especially being in college. It definitely helped in the evenings when our family would go somewhere special for dinner—as in Italy or Tokyo—or Mom would want to show me her favorite places.

But during the day, when we all had to act normal, it was the hardest.

I wanted to see places nobody had ever seen and go to countries I'd never been to, because I was definitely keeping track.

But most of all, I wanted to spend more time with Reid.

It had been a week since we'd kissed on the subway platform, and we had seen each other every day since. They were short moments, though, between school and my family, who were still getting used to me wanting to spend time with a boy.

I could see them slowly warming up to him, though, and they even invited him to dinner the next day.

The bell rang a couple minutes after my humiliation, and I hurried out the door and into the busy stream of the hallway. I usually didn't see Nella until lunch, so I made for the bathroom to grab a couple minutes of peace before my next class.

As expected, the bathroom was full of girls fixing their hair or texting. I made for the last empty stall when someone said my name.

"Sam, did you hear?" I stopped in my tracks right behind Aria. She glanced up from the mirror and the other girls around her smiled, like there was some secret I didn't know.

"Hear what?" I said, playing along.

"There's a new boy who started school today."

I should have known. Aria and her friends always went crazy over anyone new, especially in the middle of the school year. I usually tried to spot them out of the crowd, just like everyone else did, just out of curiosity. But today I found myself uninterested because I already had the only boy I could ever want.

All I said in response was "Cool."

A girl pushed past me and took the last stall. I glared at the closed door, noting the missed opportunity.

Aria turned around and cocked an eyebrow. "That's all you have to say? Come on, Sam! I just saw him before last period. He's like someone that could be a sexy lead singer of some band."

"Well, you can have him."

"Oh, I plan to." She faced the mirror again and finished applying her lip gloss. "He's going to be mine by the time this day is over."

I fought to keep my eyes from rolling. "And I'm sure you'll succeed. You always do."

The bell was about to ring, so I had no choice but to follow them out of the bathroom. I was about to head for my next class when they all stopped in front of me, blocking my way.

"Look, there he is."

I turned to see who they were looking at and my heart pounded, too hard for it to be anyone else.

Reid.

"Oh my gosh," I said, not even meaning to say it aloud.

"I know, right?" Aria touched her hair while watching Reid talk with someone next to the lockers. He was laughing at something. When he caught my eye, his smile never faded.

Then, all too fast, he was walking toward me.

A couple of books were in his hand against his hip, and he wore his black T-shirt, which I had admittedly been dreaming about. His eyes locked with mine.

"Here we go," Aria murmured next to me.

Reid stopped, eyeing me. "Fancy meeting you here," he said.

"I was about to say the same."

His dimple appeared as he closed the distance between us. It was a short, soft kiss that left my head spinning and elicited gasps from the girls next to me.

"Meet me after school," he whispered into my ear.

I could only nod as he walked past, leaving me alone, surrounded by the whispers. I didn't care about any of that.

The moment school let out, I found an empty alleyway to drift from without anyone seeing me. I didn't even care to notice where Reid was—I just drifted to him without a second thought.

He was waiting for me on the edge of a cliff in South Africa, his bag abandoned on the grass behind him.

The view was stunning from this high up, and there was a waterfall in the distance, its long white stream going all the way down to the bottom. I dropped my bag with his and approached the edge of the cliff and looked down, wondering how far it was.

"You ready to jump?" Reid asked.

I looked at him sharply. "I told you I wasn't ready for that."

"How do you know if you don't try?"

I smiled and shook my head. "Is this the only reason you brought me here? Or maybe it's a distraction because you're *going to my school*. Why didn't you tell me?"

"Because it was more fun seeing your face," Reid admitted, grinning.

He took my arm and pulled me close, and I couldn't even try to be mad at him.

"So you're going to school," I said.

"Yeah, one of the terms of staying with Jake."

"He's a smart one."

"It's just weird living like . . . I don't know." He paused, looking out across the cliffs. "Living like I was before, with my parents. Going to school, having friends, just . . . *being*."

"Is that a good thing?"

Reid looked over. "It's better than I ever thought it would be." Then he took my hand and said, "You ready for this?"

"Promise not to let go?" I asked, nerves jumping in my stomach.

"Never."

We took a running start and jumped, letting the wind carry us away.

ACKNOWLEDGMENTS

Windswept had a long and difficult journey to becoming published, and it wouldn't have happened without these few select people. So, I'm going to keep this short and sweet, otherwise it would be ten pages long and nobody would read it.

First and foremost, to my Wattpad readers. All your support, comments, and love made Windswept into what it is today. It wouldn't be here without you. Thank you.

Dad, to who this book is dedicated to, Windswept wouldn't have been published if it wasn't for your relentless dedication to bring justice. I will always know where I get my stubborn nature from.

Nicole Frail, my editor, even though it took years it finally get this book published, you never gave up on it. You were there in the beginning and you pushed me to make it the best book it could be. I'm proud to have you on my team.

Corri, as always, you are always there to read my books however many times I ask, and I appreciate you.

To my local bookstore, Chop Suey, you guys have always been supportive of me and my books and I could never thank you enough. The world needs more bookstores like you.

The Insomniacs, thank you for being the most awesome people and talking about inappropriate things at inappropriate hours.

To my family and friends, thank you for being on this ride with me. It was a crazy one.

And to the person who stole this story, thank you for making me realize it was worth fighting for.